The Red Badge of Courage

STEPHEN CRANE

SADDLEBACK
EDUCATIONAL PUBLISHING

Saddleback's *Illustrated Classics*™

SADDLEBACK
EDUCATIONAL PUBLISHING

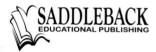

Three Watson
Irvine, CA 92618-2767
Website: www.sdlback.com

ISBN 1-56254-932-4

Printed in China

Welcome to
Saddleback's *Illustrated Classics*™

We are proud to welcome you to Saddleback's *Illustrated Classics*™. Saddleback's *Illustrated Classics*™ was designed specifically for the classroom to introduce readers to many of the great classics in literature. Each text, written and adapted by teachers and researchers, has been edited using the Dale-Chall vocabulary system. In addition, much time and effort has been spent to ensure that these high-interest stories retain all of the excitement, intrigue, and adventure of the original books.

With these graphically *Illustrated Classics*™, you learn what happens in the story in a number of different ways. One way is by reading the words a character says. Another way is by looking at the drawings of the character. The artist can tell you what kind of person a character is and what he or she is thinking or feeling.

This series will help you to develop confidence and a sense of accomplishment as you finish each novel. The stories in Saddleback's *Illustrated Classics*™ are fun to read. And remember, fun motivates!

Overview

Everyone deserves to read the best literature our language has to offer. Saddleback's *Illustrated Classics*™ was designed to acquaint readers with the most famous stories from the world's greatest authors, while teaching essential skills. You will learn how to:

- Establish a purpose for reading
- Use prior knowledge
- Evaluate your reading
- Listen to the language as it is written
- Extend literary and language appreciation through discussion and writing activities

Reading is one of the most important skills you will ever learn. It provides the key to all kinds of information. By reading the *Illustrated Classics*™, you will develop confidence and the self-satisfaction that comes from accomplishment—a solid foundation for any reader.

Step-By-Step

The following is a simple guide to using and enjoying each of your *Illustrated Classics*™. To maximize your use of the learning activities provided, we suggest that you follow these steps:

1. ***Listen!*** We suggest that you listen to the read-along. (At this time, please ignore the beeps.) You will enjoy this wonderfully dramatized presentation.

2. ***Pre-reading Activities.*** After listening to the audio presentation, the pre-reading activities in the Activity Book prepare you for reading the story by setting the scene, introducing more difficult vocabulary words, and providing some short exercises.

3. ***Reading Activities.*** Now turn to the "While you are reading" portion of the Activity Book, which directs you to make a list of story-related facts. Read-along while listening to the audio presentation. (This time pay attention to the beeps, as they indicate when each page should be turned.)

4. ***Post-reading Activities.*** You have successfully read the story and listened to the audio presentation. Now answer the multiple-choice questions and other activities in the Activity Book.

Remember,

"Today's readers are tomorrow's leaders."

Stephen Crane

Stephen Crane, an American novelist, short-story writer, poet, and journalist, was born in Newark, New Jersey in 1871. The 14th child in his family, he briefly attended college, but left to work as a newspaper writer in New York City.

Work as a war correspondent later took Crane to Greece, Cuba, and Mexico. On one trip his boat was shipwrecked, and he and his fellow passengers spent four days adrift at sea before they were rescued.

Like many writers, Crane drew on his experiences in his work. His observations of New York City's slums were the basis for his first novel. The frightening shipwreck episode became his great short story, "The Open Boat." But his most famous novel, *The Red Badge of Courage: An Episode of the American Civil War,* was based on conversations with war veterans, historic accounts of military battles, and his own vivid imagination. It was not until after it was published that Crane, the war correspondent, saw the horrors he had so movingly described.

Crane died of tuberculosis in 1900. Although he was only 28 when he died, he left a large and pioneering body of work.

Saddleback's *Illustrated Classics*™

The Red Badge of Courage

STEPHEN CRANE

THE MAIN CHARACTERS

Mother

Jim Conklin

Henry Fleming

Wilson

General

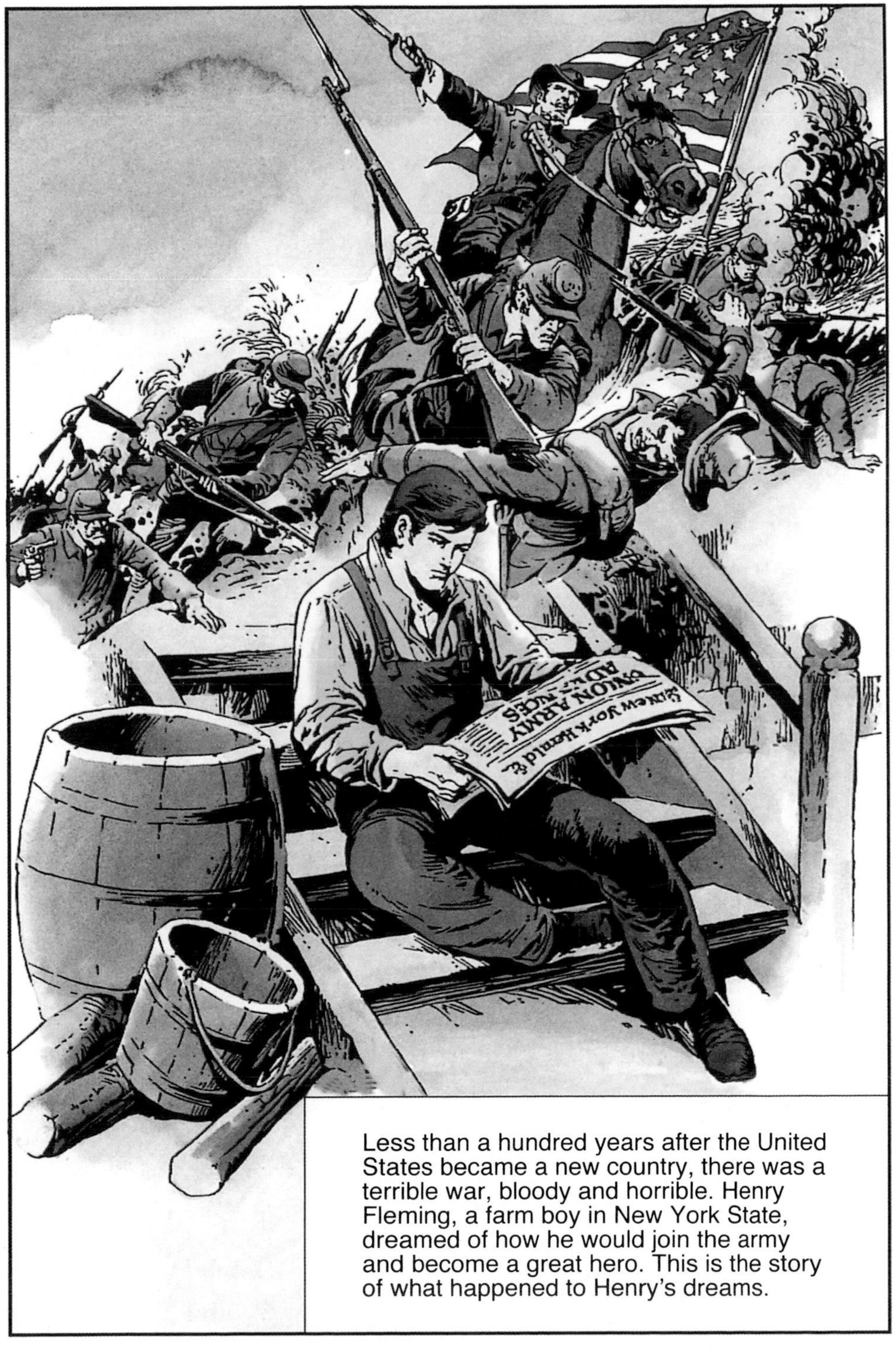
New York Herald
UNION ARMY
Less than a hundred years after the United States became a new country, there was a terrible war, bloody and horrible. Henry Fleming, a farm boy in New York State, dreamed of how he would join the army and become a great hero. This is the story of what happened to Henry's dreams.

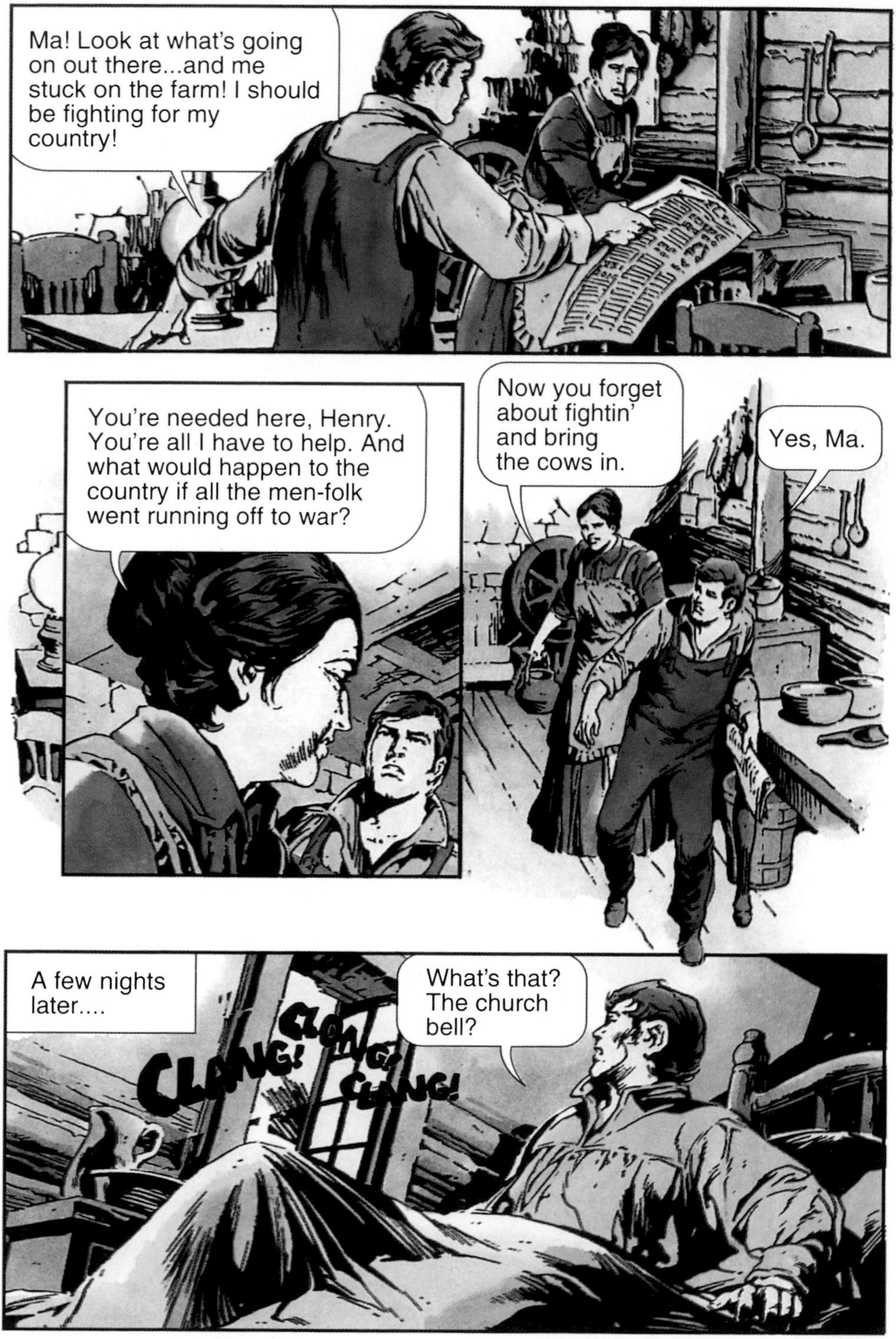
Ma! Look at what's going on out there...and me stuck on the farm! I should be fighting for my country!
You're needed here, Henry. You're all I have to help. And what would happen to the country if all the men-folk went running off to war?
Now you forget about fightin' and bring the cows in.
Yes, Ma.
A few nights later....
CLANG!
CLANG!
CLANG!
CLANG!
What's that? The church bell?

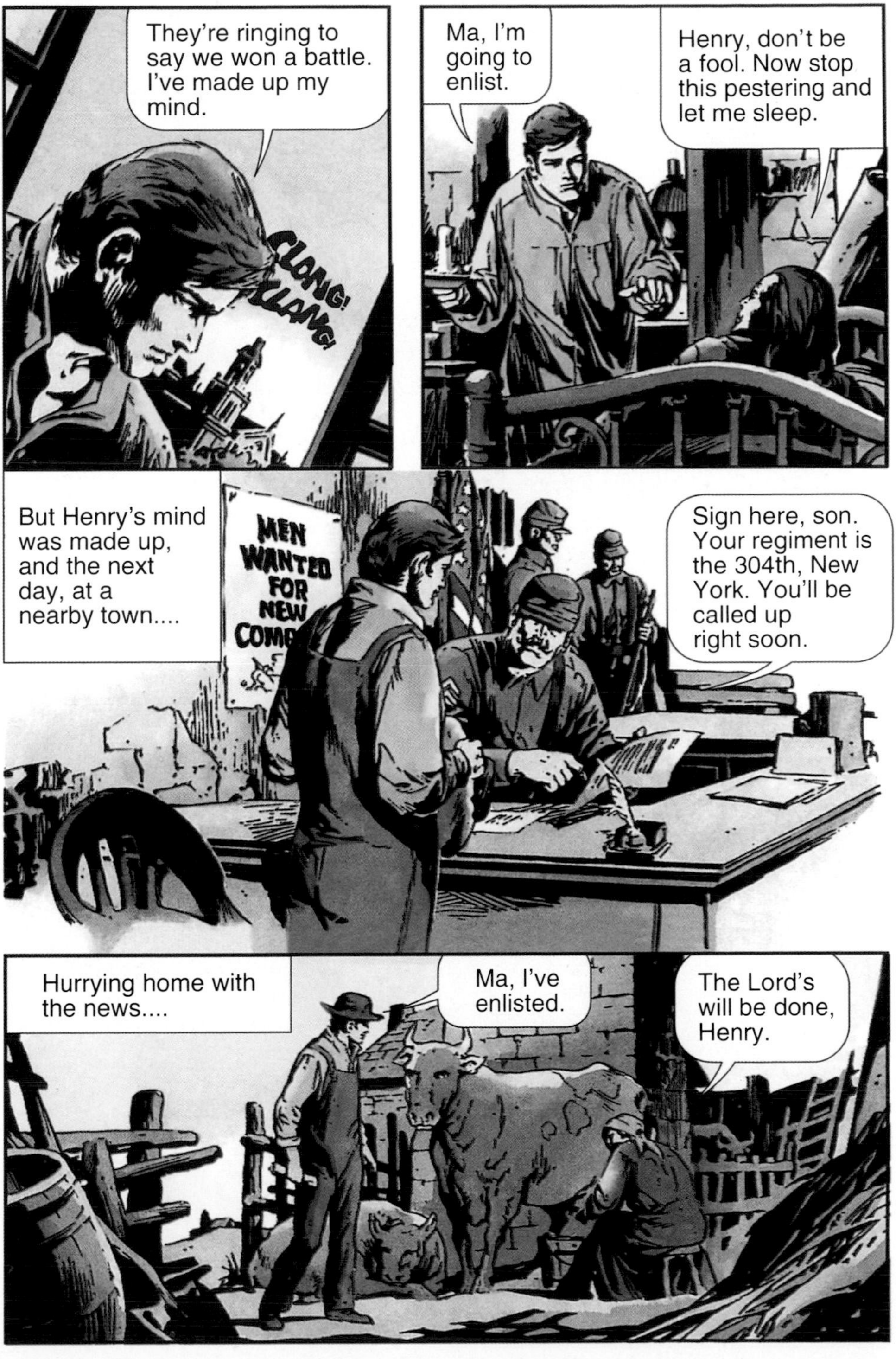
They're ringing to say we won a battle. I've made up my mind.
CLONG! CLANG!
Ma, I'm going to enlist.
Henry, don't be a fool. Now stop this pestering and let me sleep.
But Henry's mind was made up, and the next day, at a nearby town....
MEN WANTED FOR NEW
Sign here, son. Your regiment is the 304th, New York. You'll be called up right soon.
Hurrying home with the news....
Ma, I've enlisted.
The Lord's will be done, Henry.

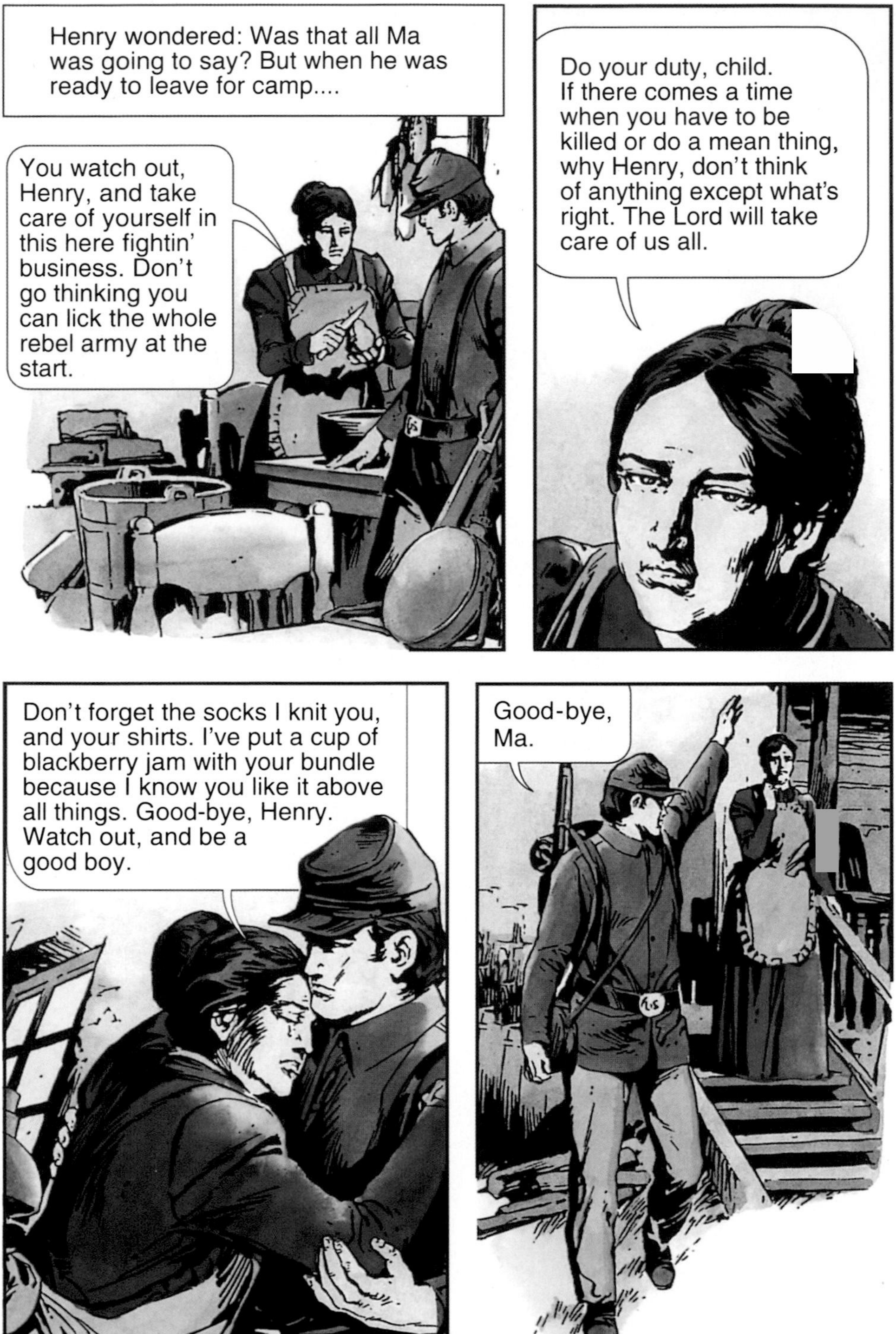
Henry wondered: Was that all Ma was going to say? But when he was ready to leave for camp....
You watch out, Henry, and take care of yourself in this here fightin' business. Don't go thinking you can lick the whole rebel army at the start.
Do your duty, child. If there comes a time when you have to be killed or do a mean thing, why Henry, don't think of anything except what's right. The Lord will take care of us all.
Don't forget the socks I knit you, and your shirts. I've put a cup of blackberry jam with your bundle because I know you like it above all things. Good-bye, Henry. Watch out, and be a good boy.
Good-bye, Ma.

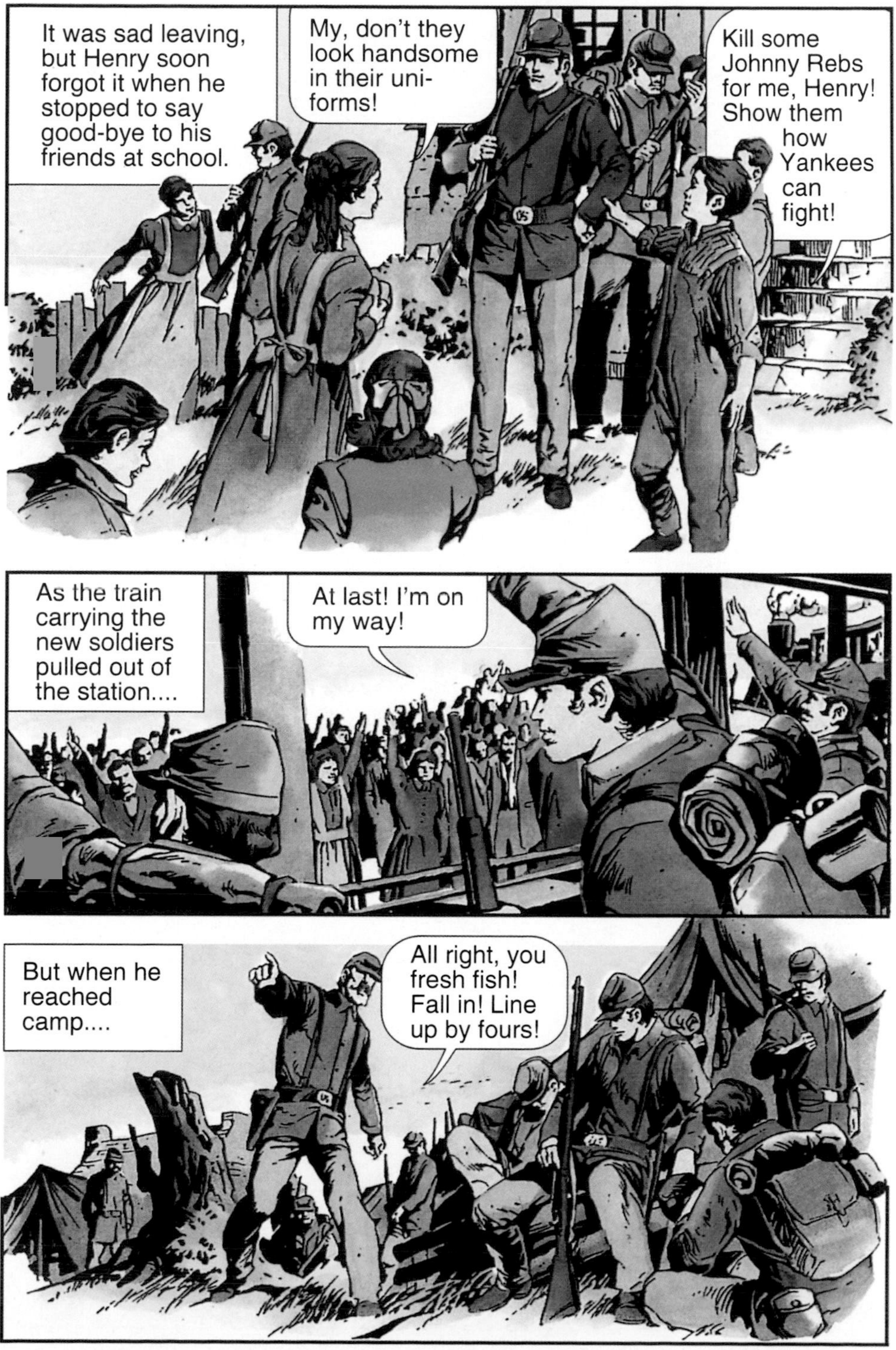
It was sad leaving, but Henry soon forgot it when he stopped to say good-bye to his friends at school.
My, don't they look handsome in their uni-forms!
Kill some Johnny Rebs for me, Henry! Show them how Yankees can fight!
As the train carrying the new soldiers pulled out of the station....
At last! I'm on my way!
But when he reached camp....
All right, you fresh fish! Fall in! Line up by fours!

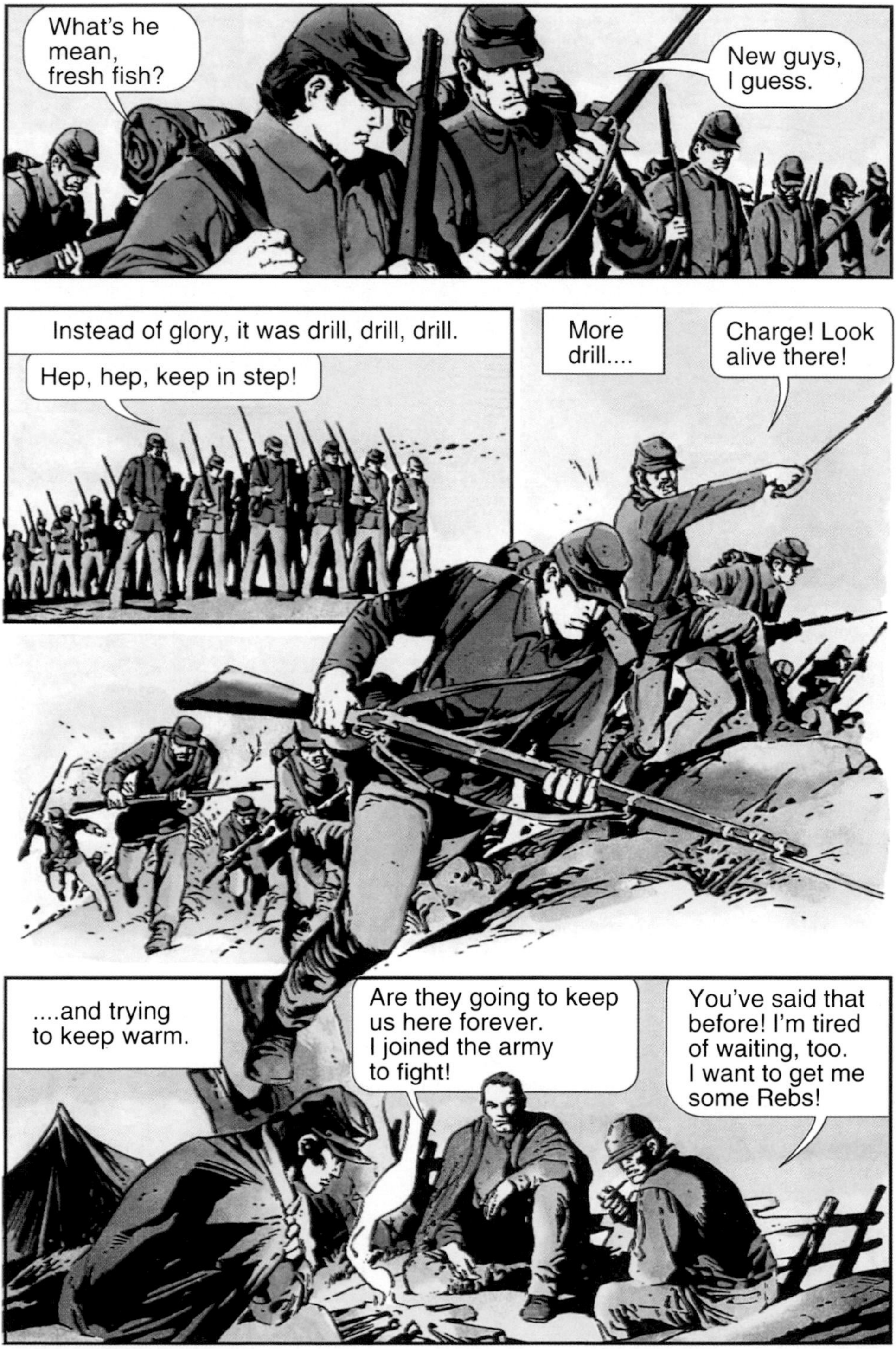
What's he mean, fresh fish?
New guys, I guess.
Instead of glory, it was drill, drill, drill.
Hep, hep, keep in step!
More drill....
Charge! Look alive there!
....and trying to keep warm.
Are they going to keep us here forever. I joined the army to fight!
You've said that before! I'm tired of waiting, too. I want to get me some Rebs!

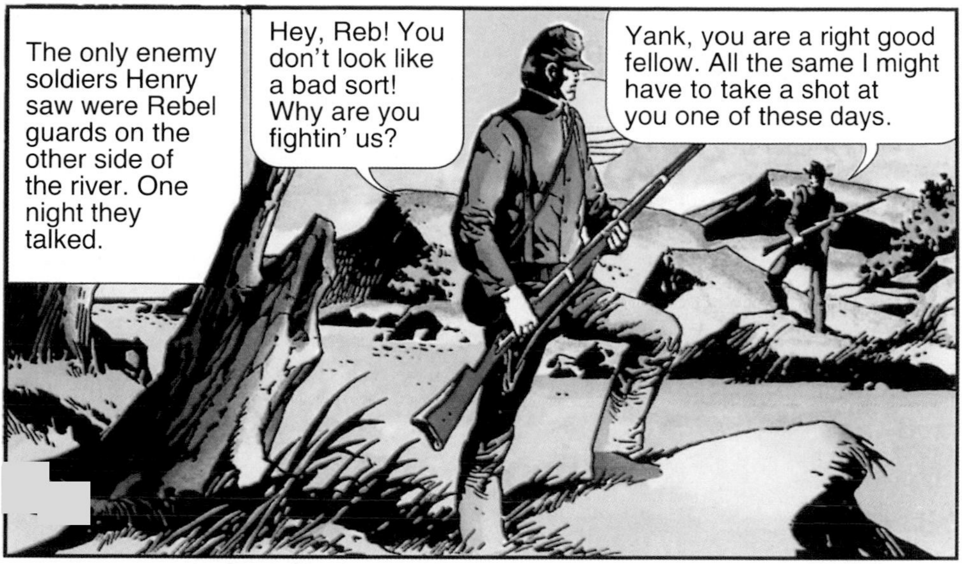
The only enemy soldiers Henry saw were Rebel guards on the other side of the river. One night they talked.
Hey, Reb! You don't look like a bad sort! Why are you fightin' us?
Yank, you are a right good fellow. All the same I might have to take a shot at you one of these days.

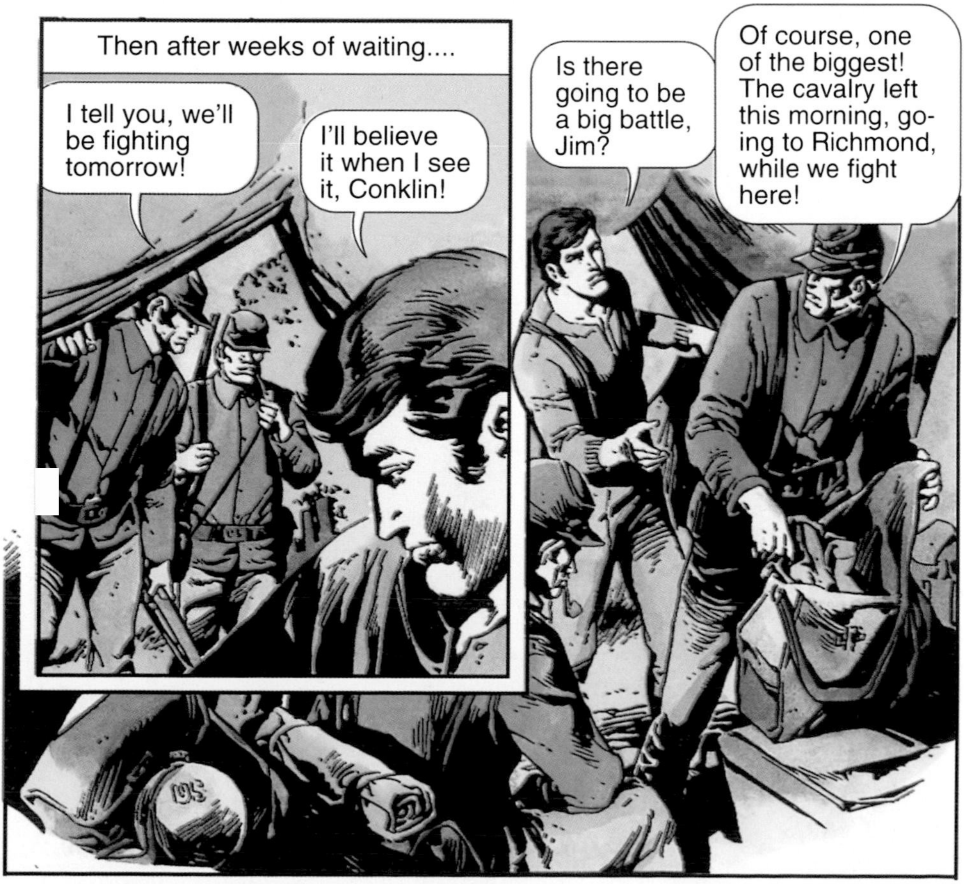
Then after weeks of waiting....
I tell you, we'll be fighting tomorrow!
I'll believe it when I see it, Conklin!
Is there going to be a big battle, Jim?
Of course, one of the biggest! The cavalry left this morning, going to Richmond, while we fight here!

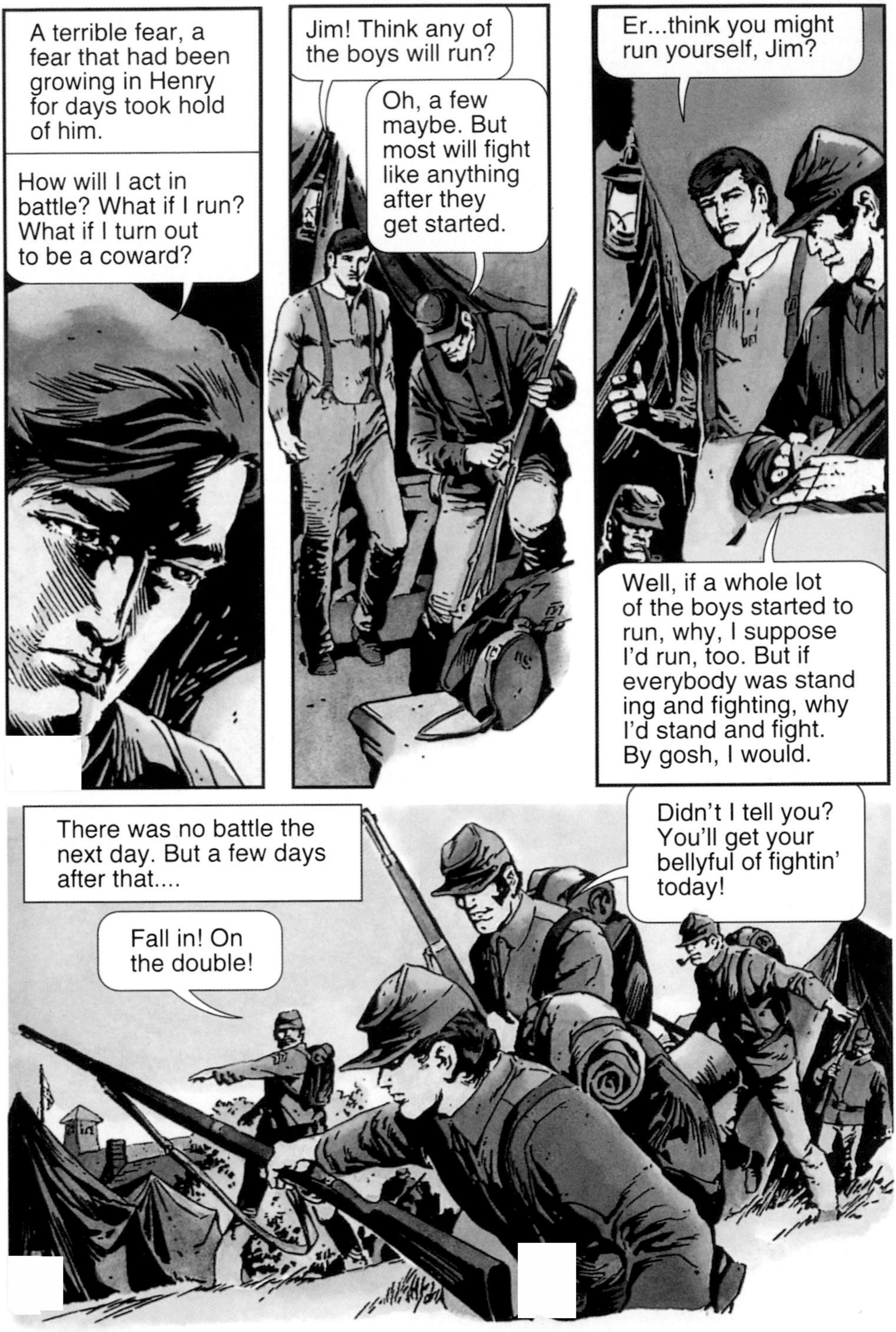
A terrible fear, a fear that had been growing in Henry for days took hold of him.
How will I act in battle? What if I run? What if I turn out to be a coward?
Jim! Think any of the boys will run?
Oh, a few maybe. But most will fight like anything after they get started.
Er...think you might run yourself, Jim?
Well, if a whole lot of the boys started to run, why, I suppose I'd run, too. But if everybody was stand ing and fighting, why I'd stand and fight. By gosh, I would.
There was no battle the next day. But a few days after that....
Fall in! On the double!
Didn't I tell you? You'll get your bellyful of fightin' today!

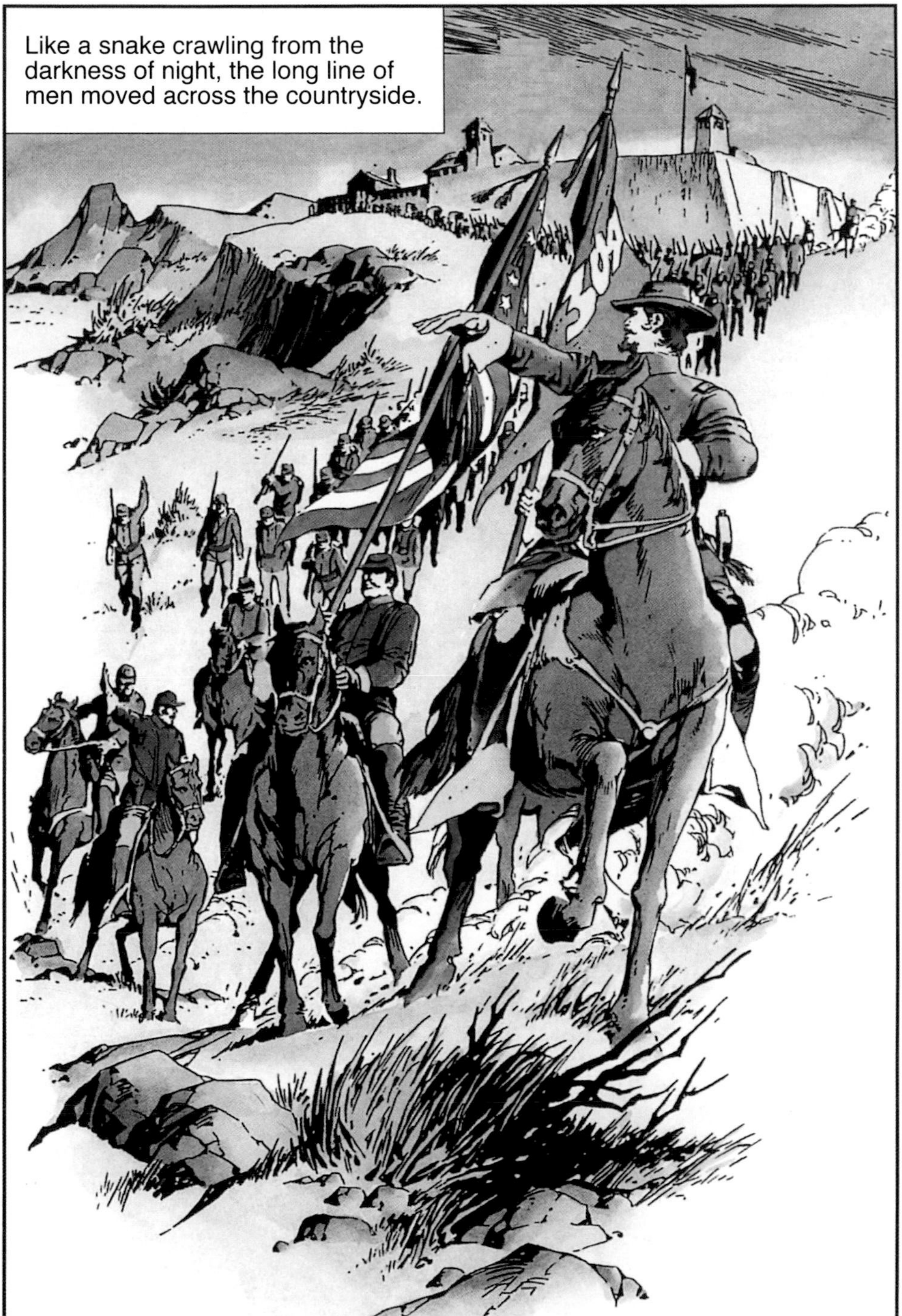
Like a snake crawling from the darkness of night, the long line of men moved across the countryside.

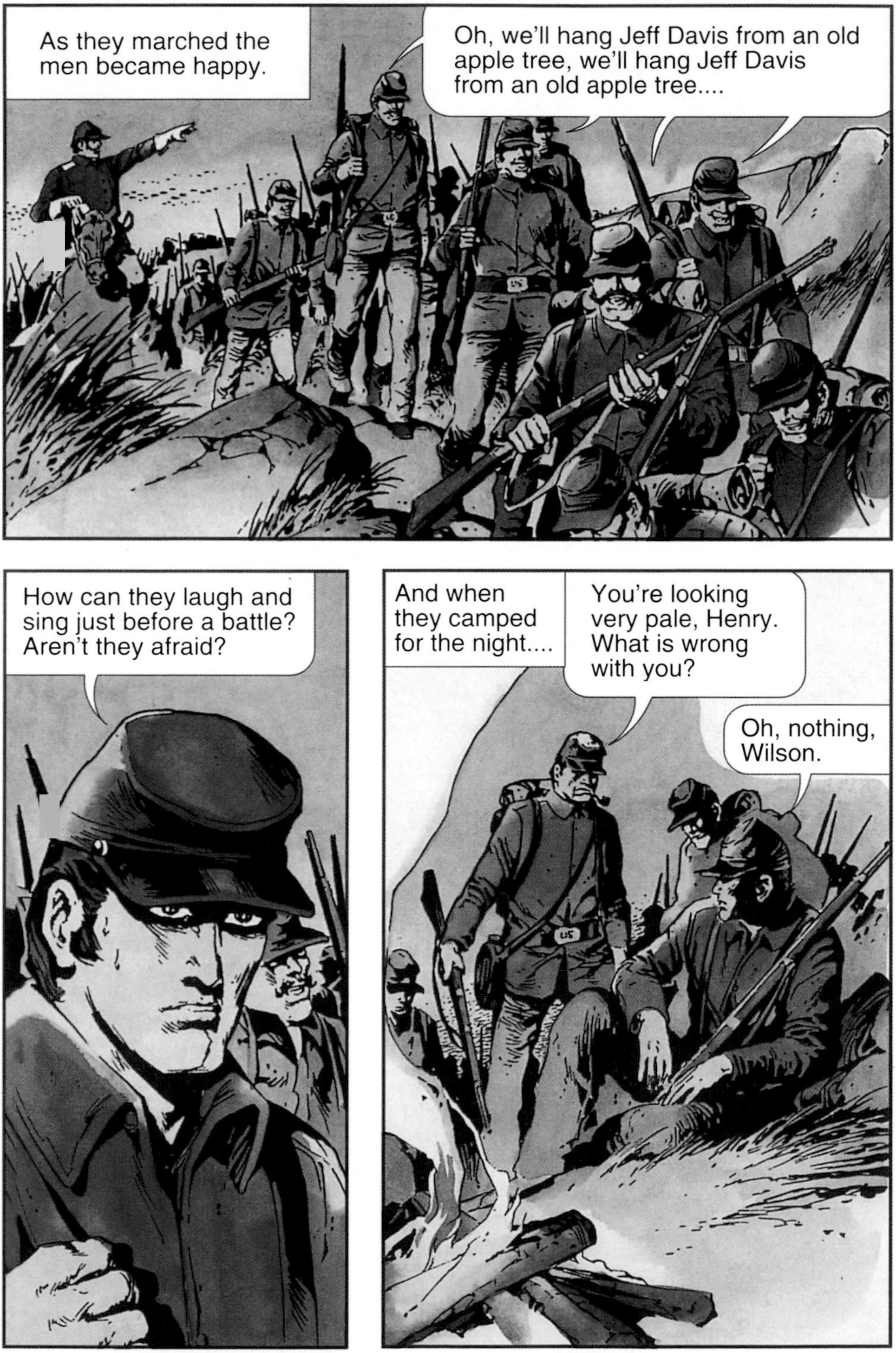
As they marched the men became happy.
Oh, we'll hang Jeff Davis from an old apple tree, we'll hang Jeff Davis from an old apple tree....
How can they laugh and sing just before a battle? Aren't they afraid?
And when they camped for the night....
You're looking very pale, Henry. What is wrong with you?
Oh, nothing, Wilson.

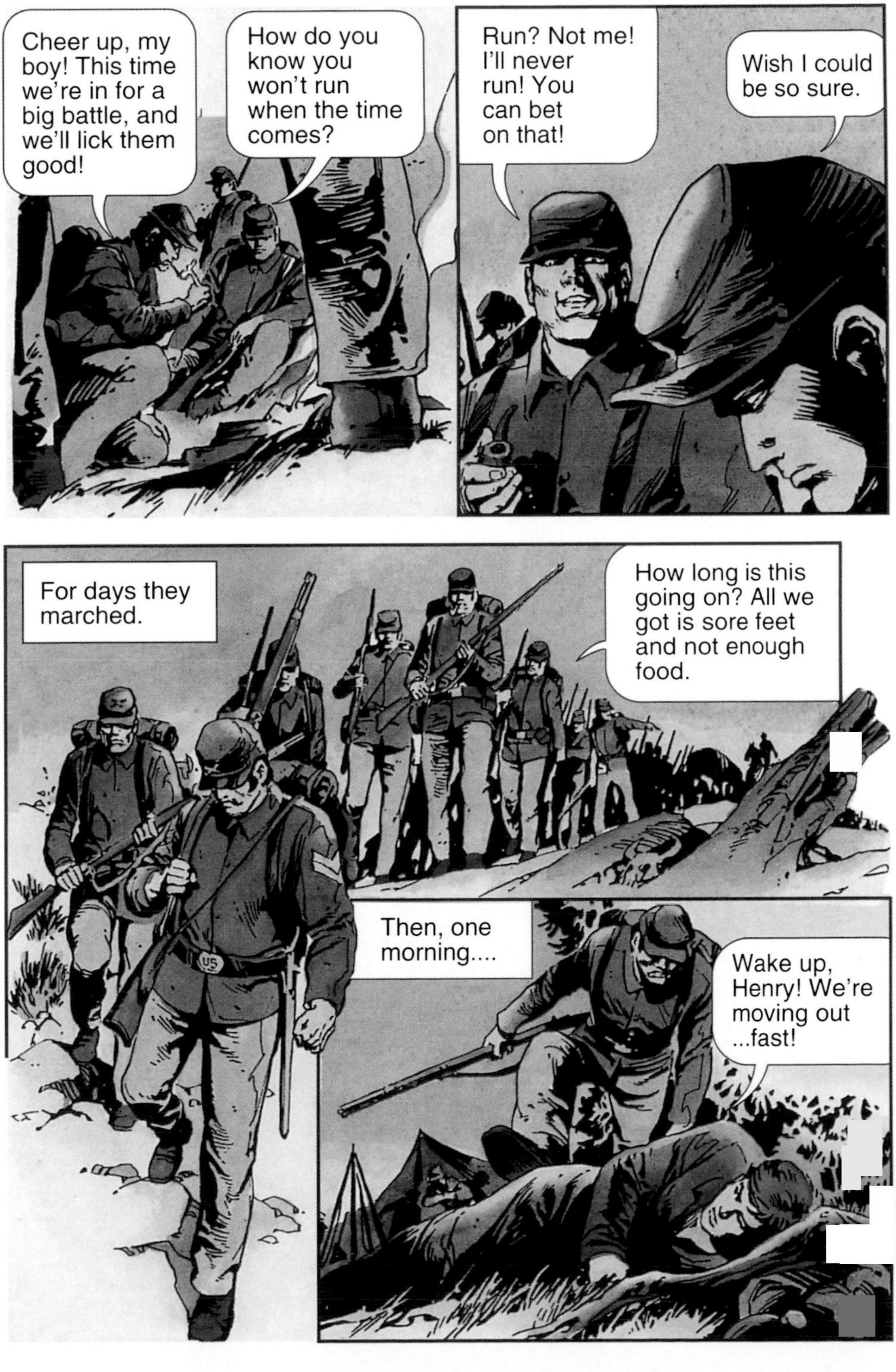
Cheer up, my boy! This time we're in for a big battle, and we'll lick them good!
How do you know you won't run when the time comes?
Run? Not me! I'll never run! You can bet on that!
Wish I could be so sure.
For days they marched.
How long is this going on? All we got is sore feet and not enough food.
Then, one morning....
Wake up, Henry! We're moving out ...fast!

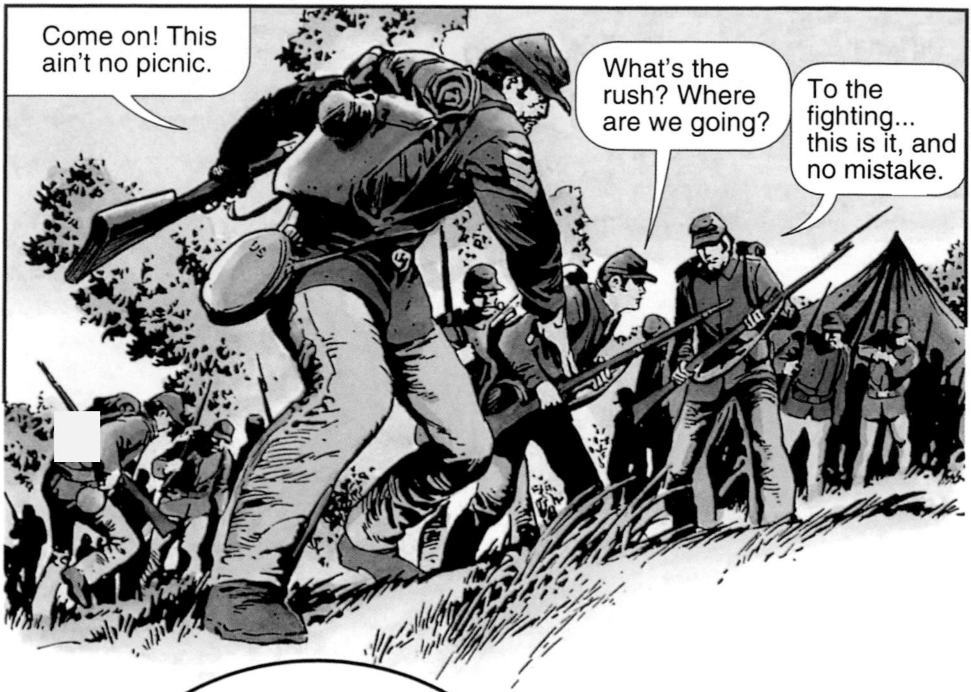
Come on! This ain't no picnic.
What's the rush? Where are we going?
To the fighting... this is it, and no mistake.

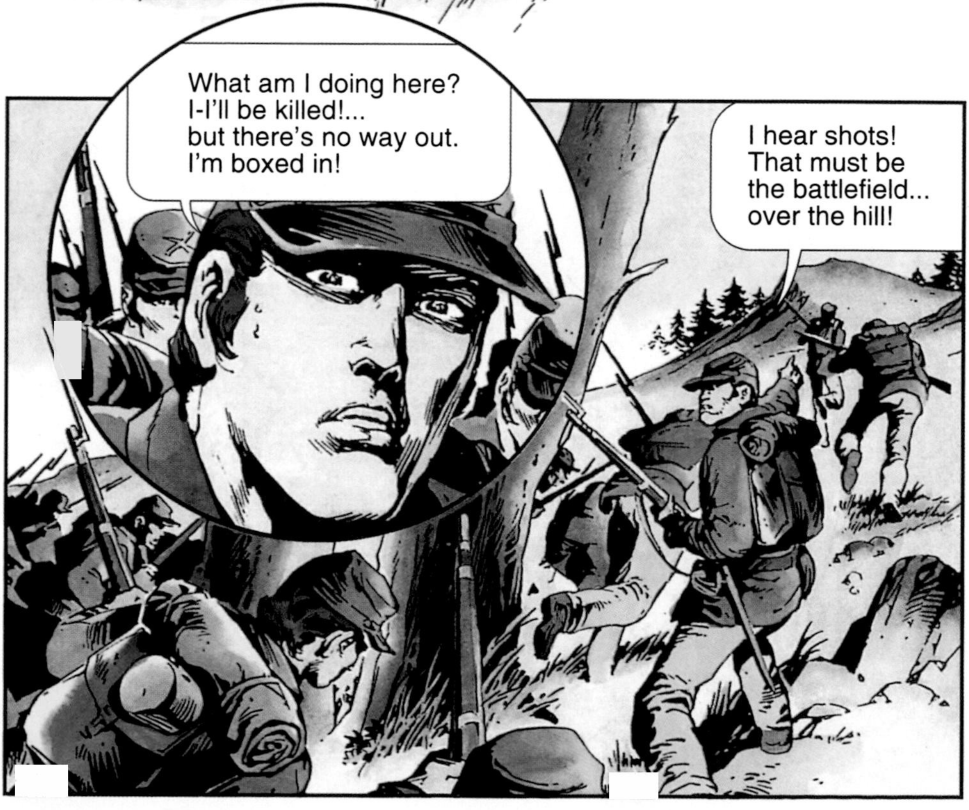
What am I doing here? I-I'll be killed!... but there's no way out. I'm boxed in!
I hear shots! That must be the battlefield... over the hill!

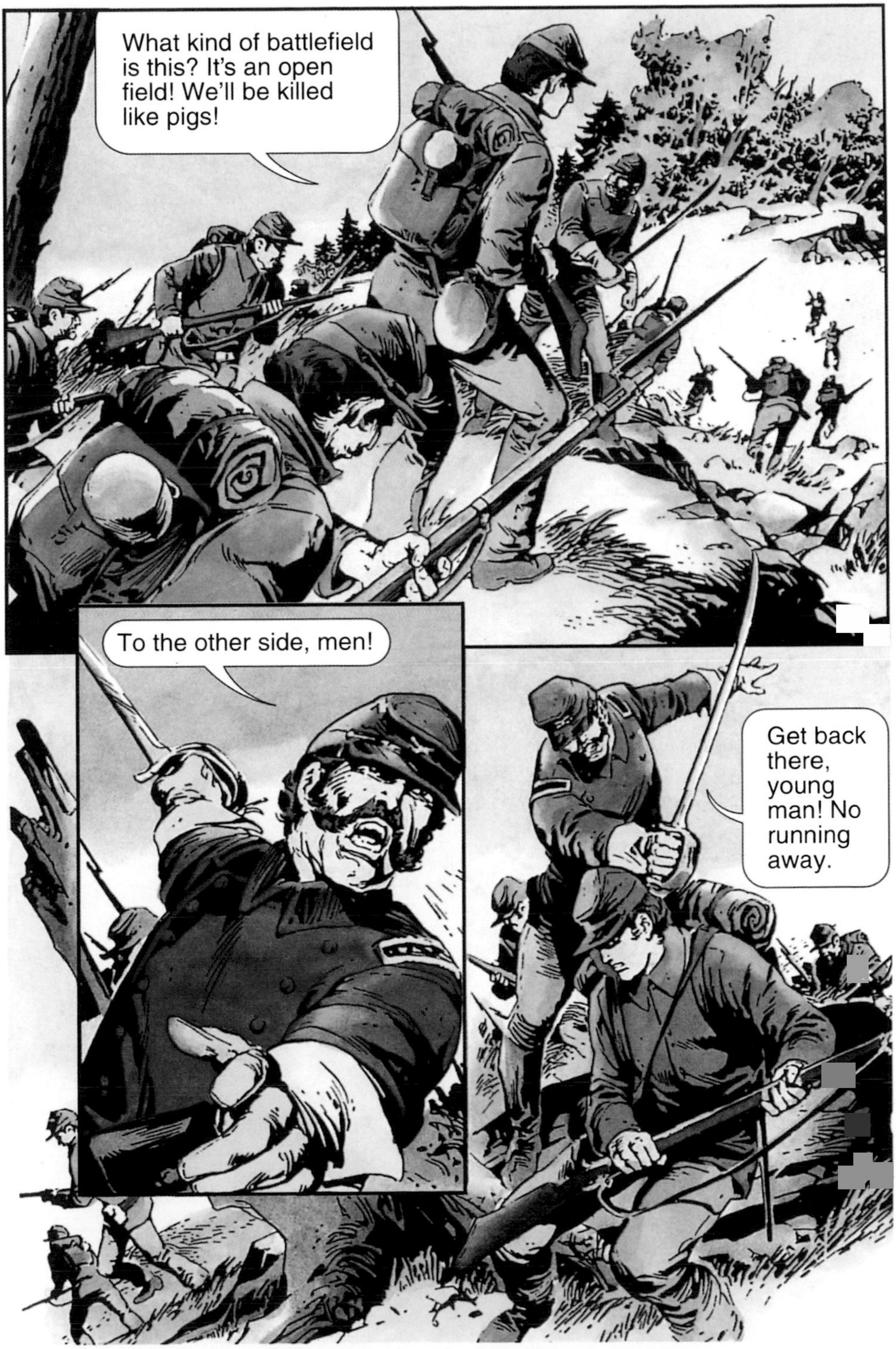
What kind of battlefield is this? It's an open field! We'll be killed like pigs!
To the other side, men!
Get back there, young man! No running away.

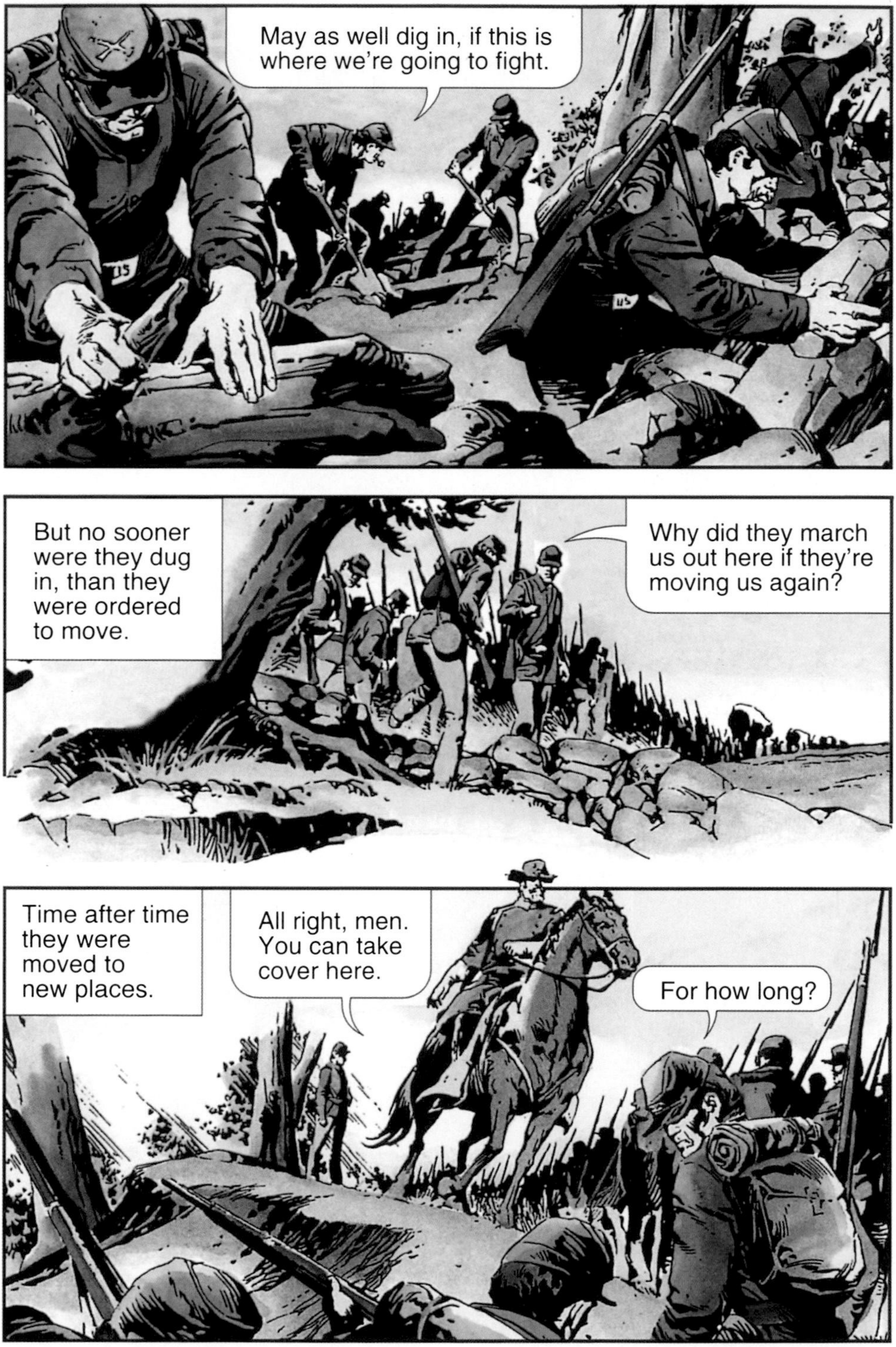
May as well dig in, if this is where we're going to fight.
But no sooner were they dug in, than they were ordered to move.
Why did they march us out here if they're moving us again?
Time after time they were moved to new places.
All right, men. You can take cover here.
For how long?

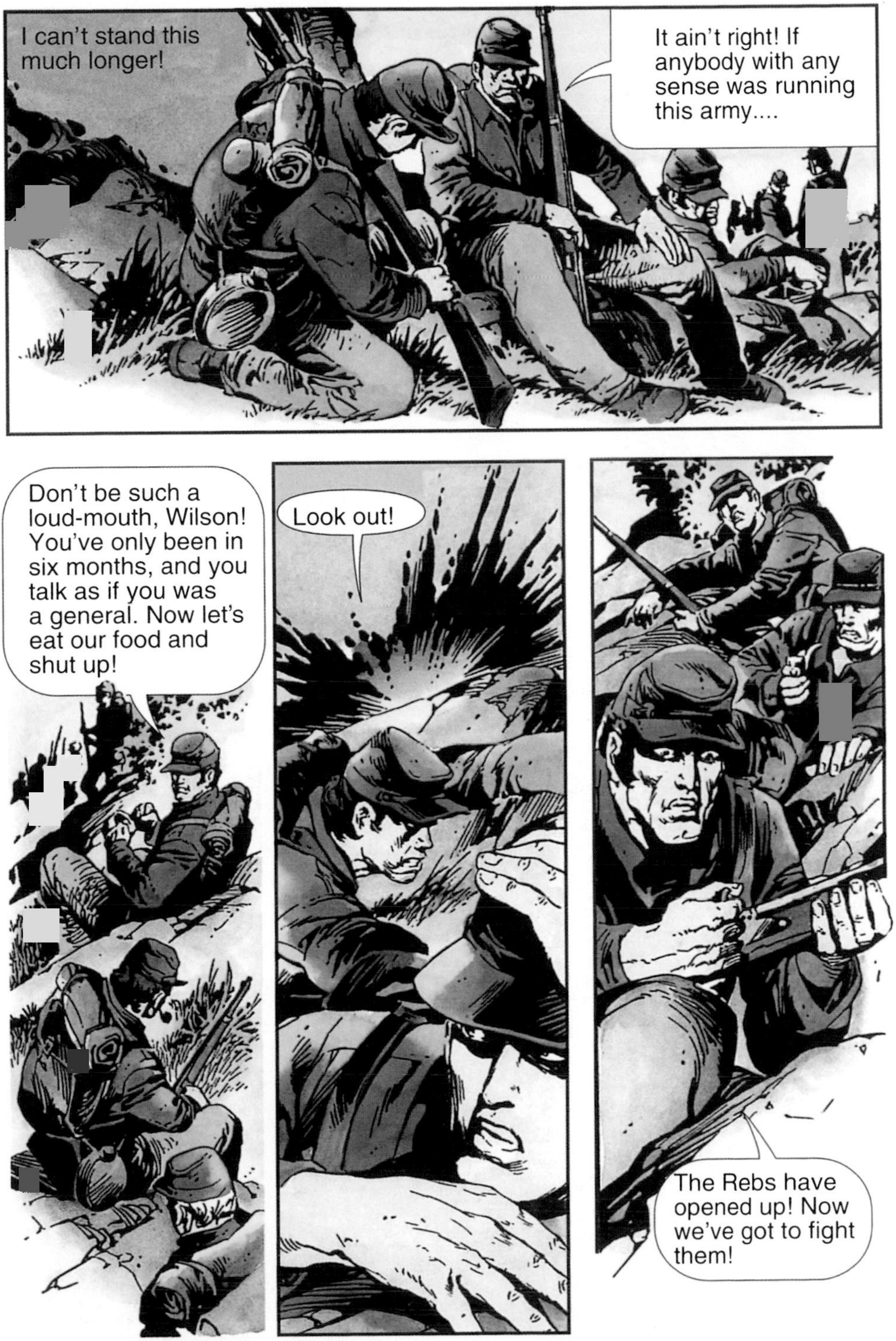
I can't stand this much longer!
It ain't right! If anybody with any sense was running this army....
Don't be such a loud-mouth, Wilson! You've only been in six months, and you talk as if you was a general. Now let's eat our food and shut up!
Look out!
The Rebs have opened up! Now we've got to fight them!

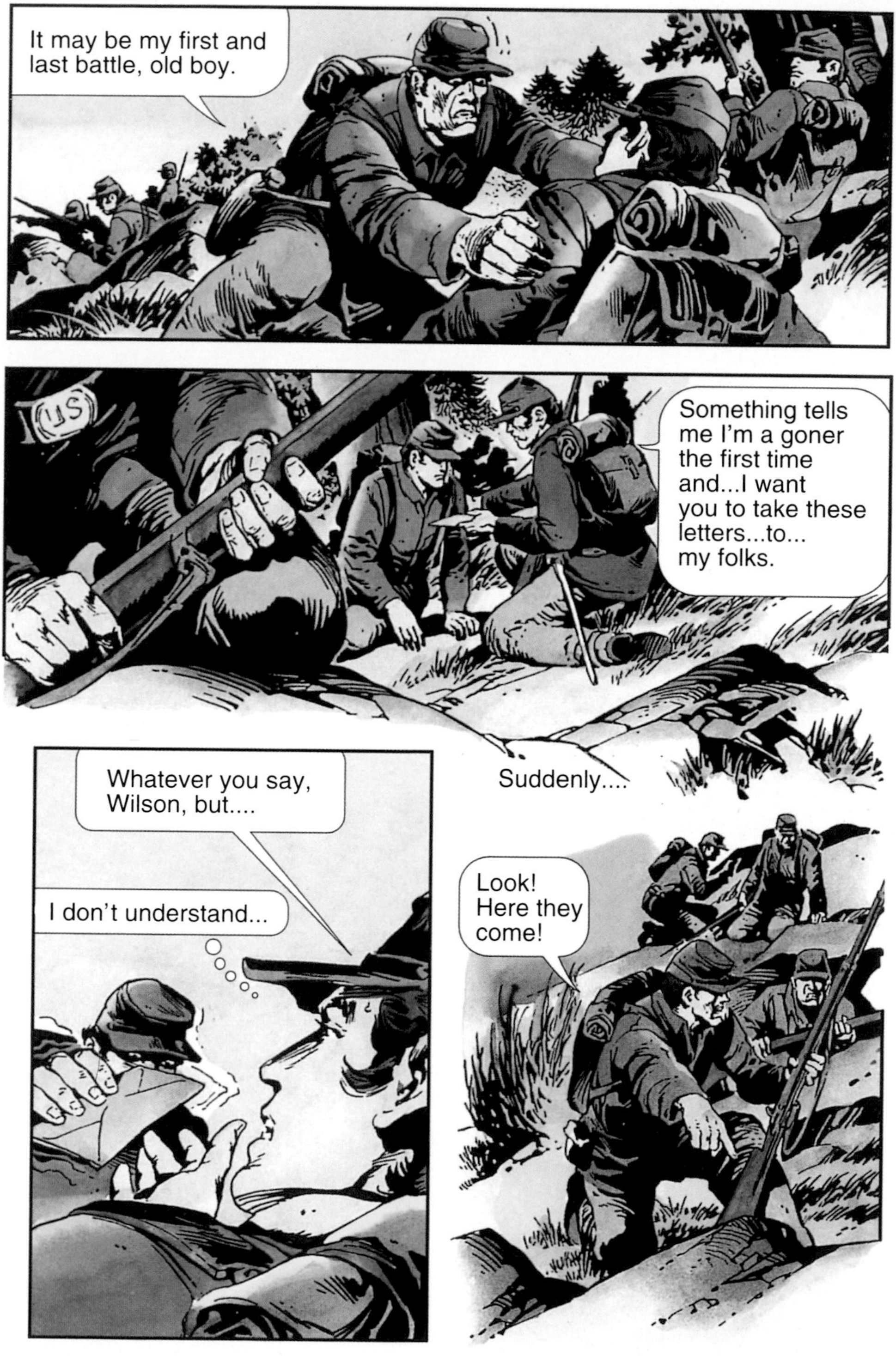
It may be my first and last battle, old boy.
Something tells me I'm a goner the first time and...I want you to take these letters...to... my folks.
Whatever you say, Wilson, but....
I don't understand...
Suddenly....
Look! Here they come!

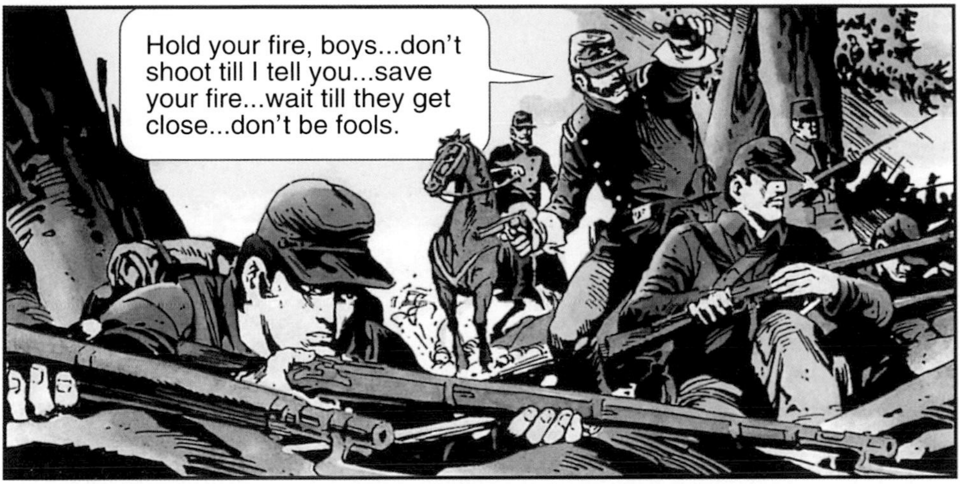
Hold your fire, boys...don't shoot till I tell you...save your fire...wait till they get close...don't be fools.

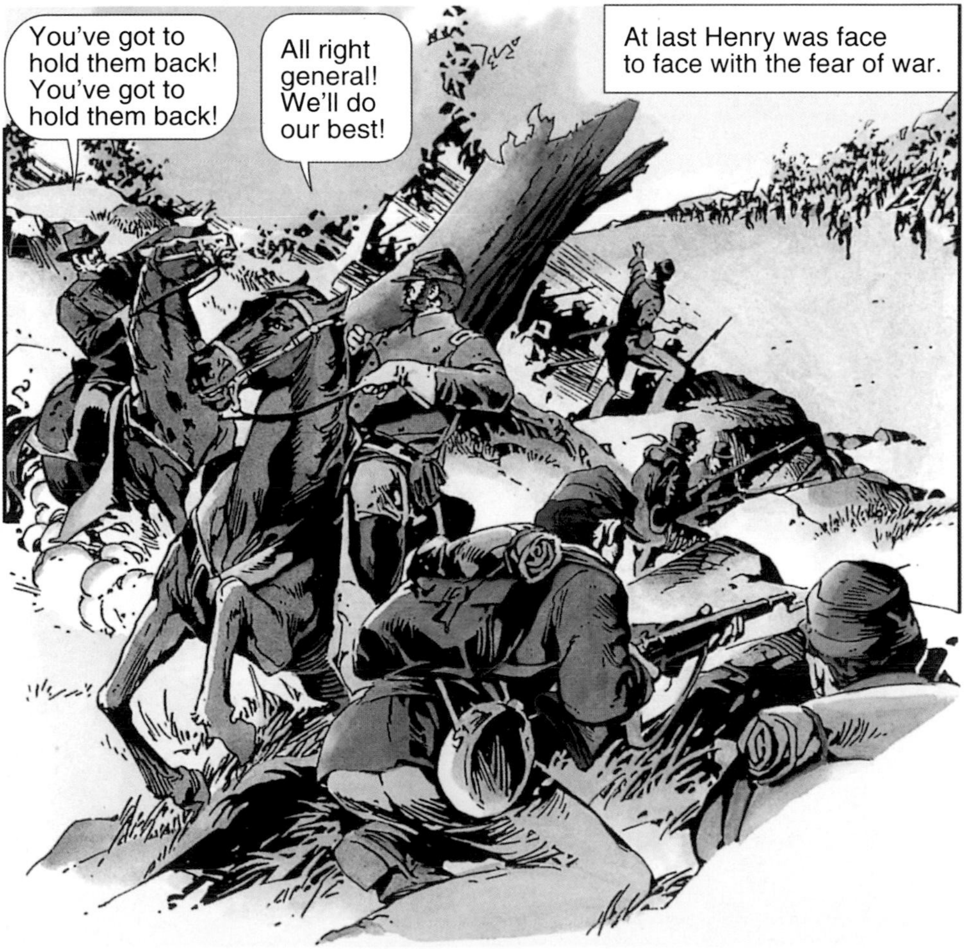
You've got to hold them back! You've got to hold them back!
All right general! We'll do our best!
At last Henry was face to face with the fear of war.

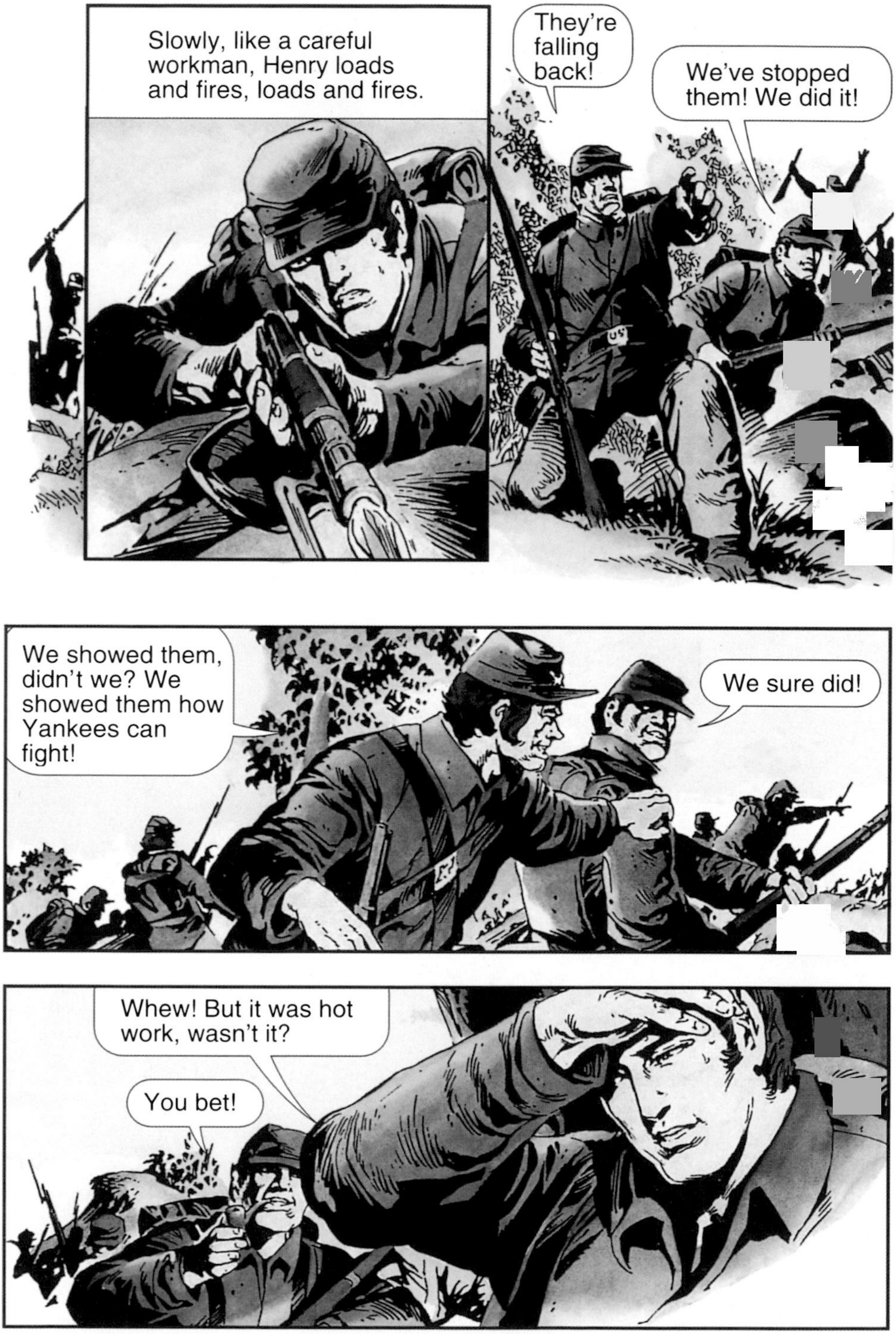

Slowly, like a careful workman, Henry loads and fires, loads and fires.
They're falling back!
We've stopped them! We did it!
We showed them, didn't we? We showed them how Yankees can fight!
We sure did!
Whew! But it was hot work, wasn't it?
You bet!

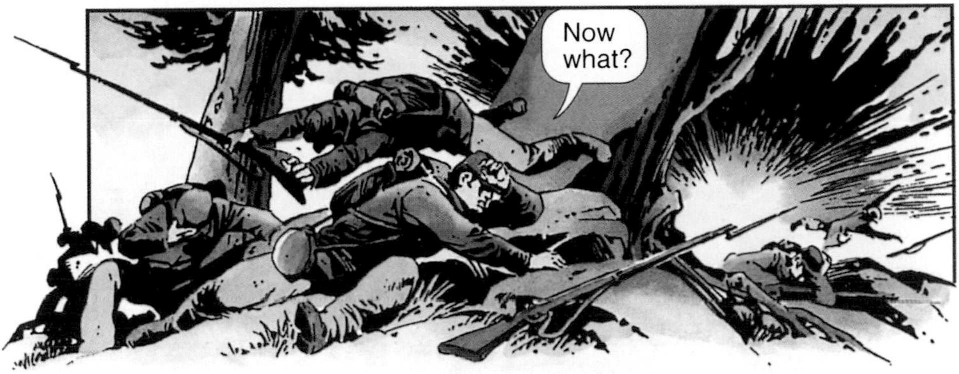
Now what?

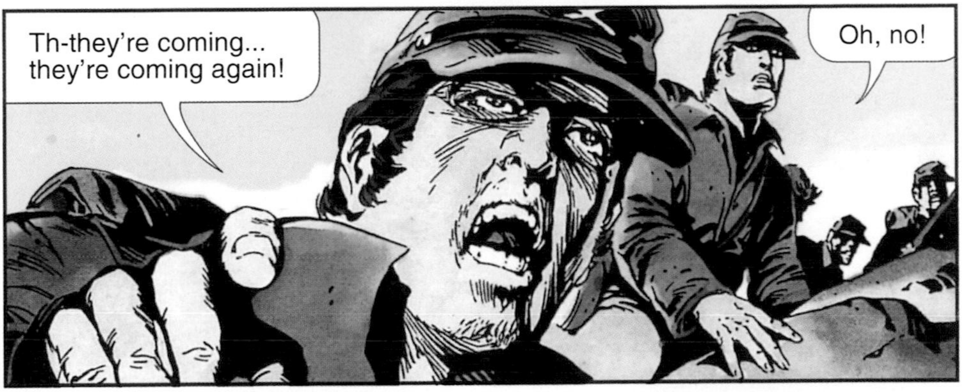
Th-they're coming... they're coming again!
Oh, no!

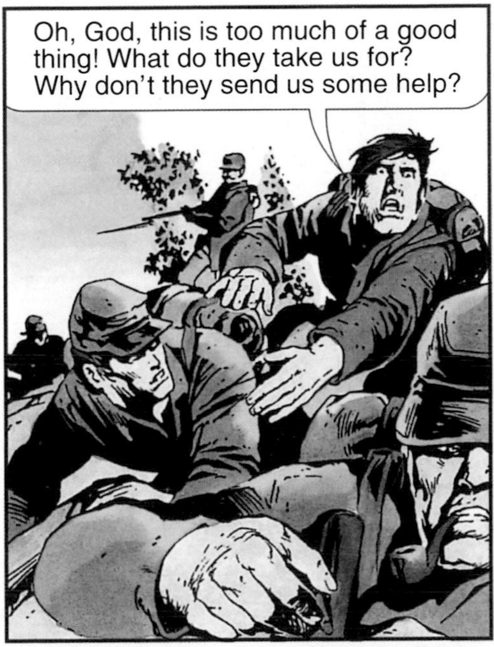
Oh, God, this is too much of a good thing! What do they take us for? Why don't they send us some help?

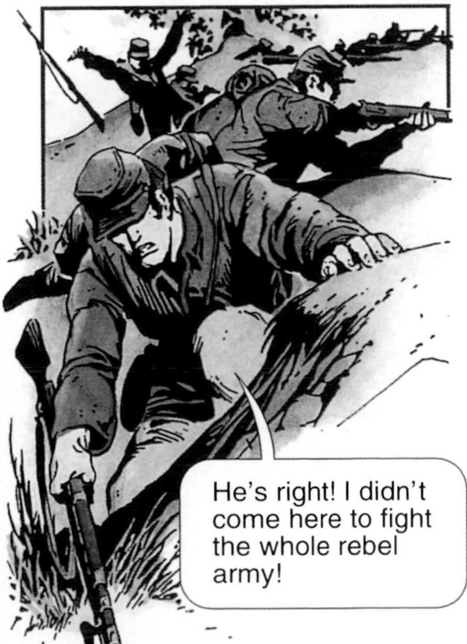
He's right! I didn't come here to fight the whole rebel army!

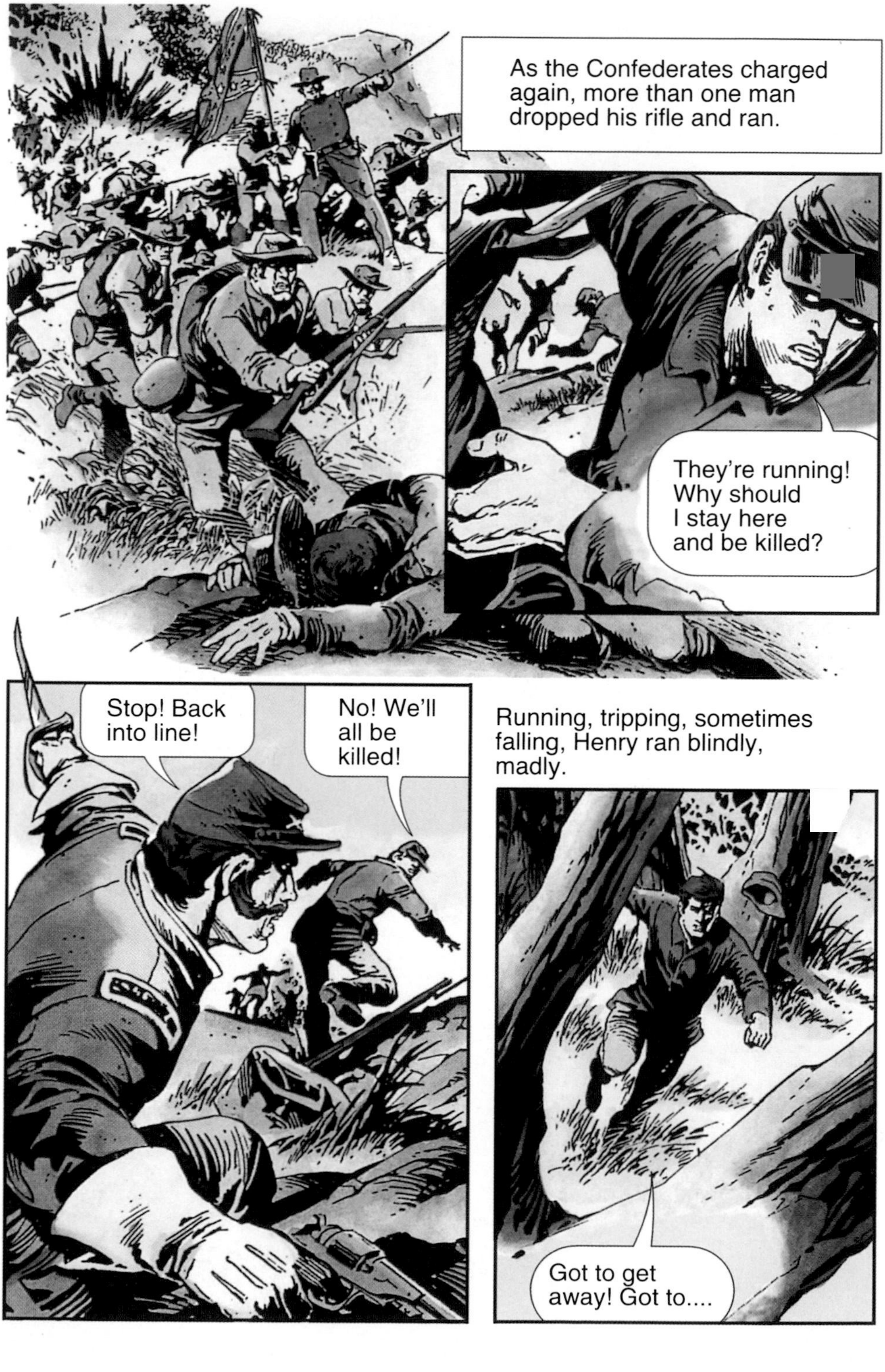
As the Confederates charged again, more than one man dropped his rifle and ran.
They're running! Why should I stay here and be killed?
Stop! Back into line!
No! We'll all be killed!
Running, tripping, sometimes falling, Henry ran blindly, madly.
Got to get away! Got to....

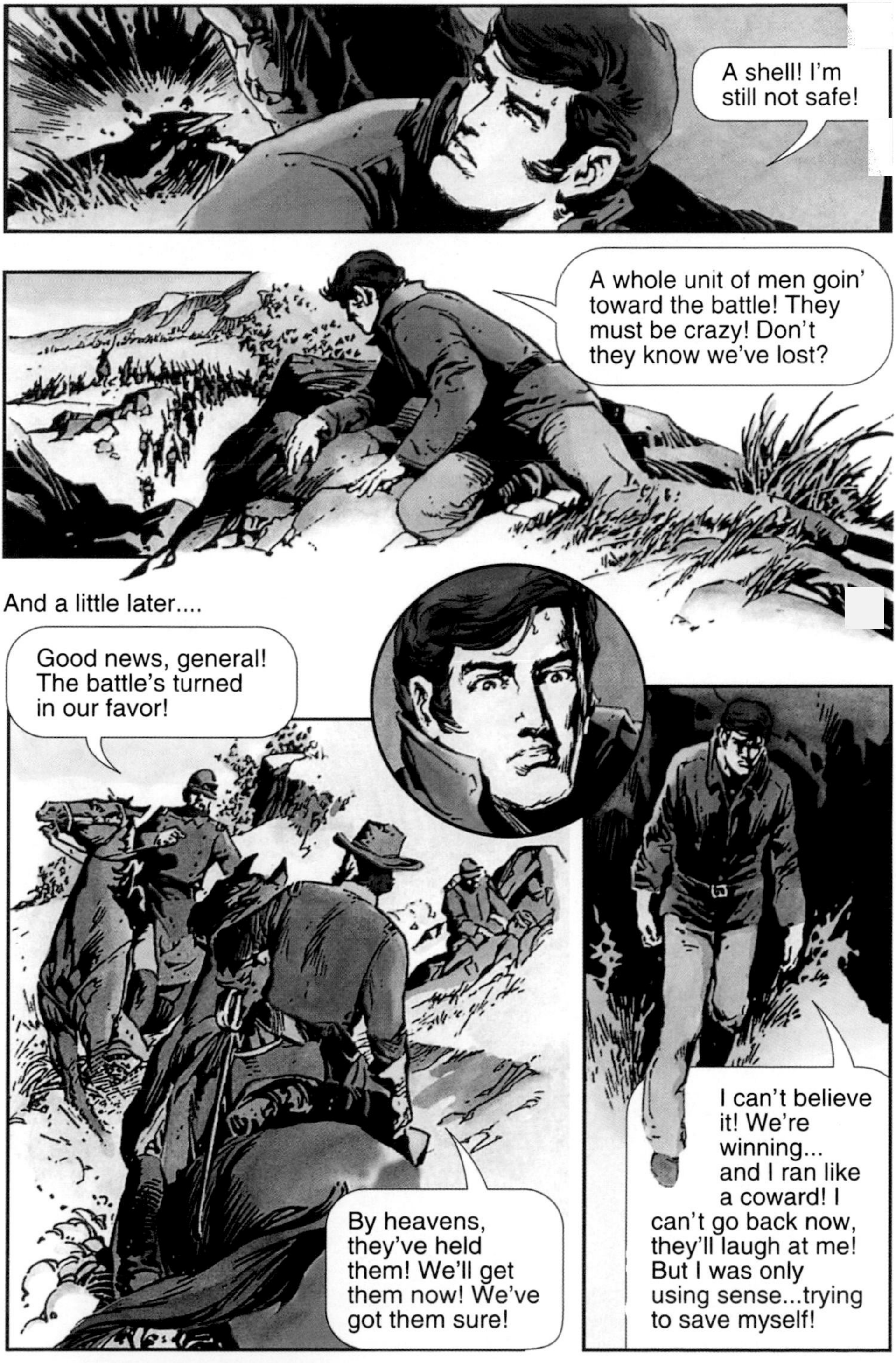
A shell! I'm still not safe!
A whole unit of men goin' toward the battle! They must be crazy! Don't they know we've lost?
And a little later....
Good news, general! The battle's turned in our favor!
By heavens, they've held them! We'll get them now! We've got them sure!
I can't believe it! We're winning... and I ran like a coward! I can't go back now, they'll laugh at me! But I was only using sense...trying to save myself!

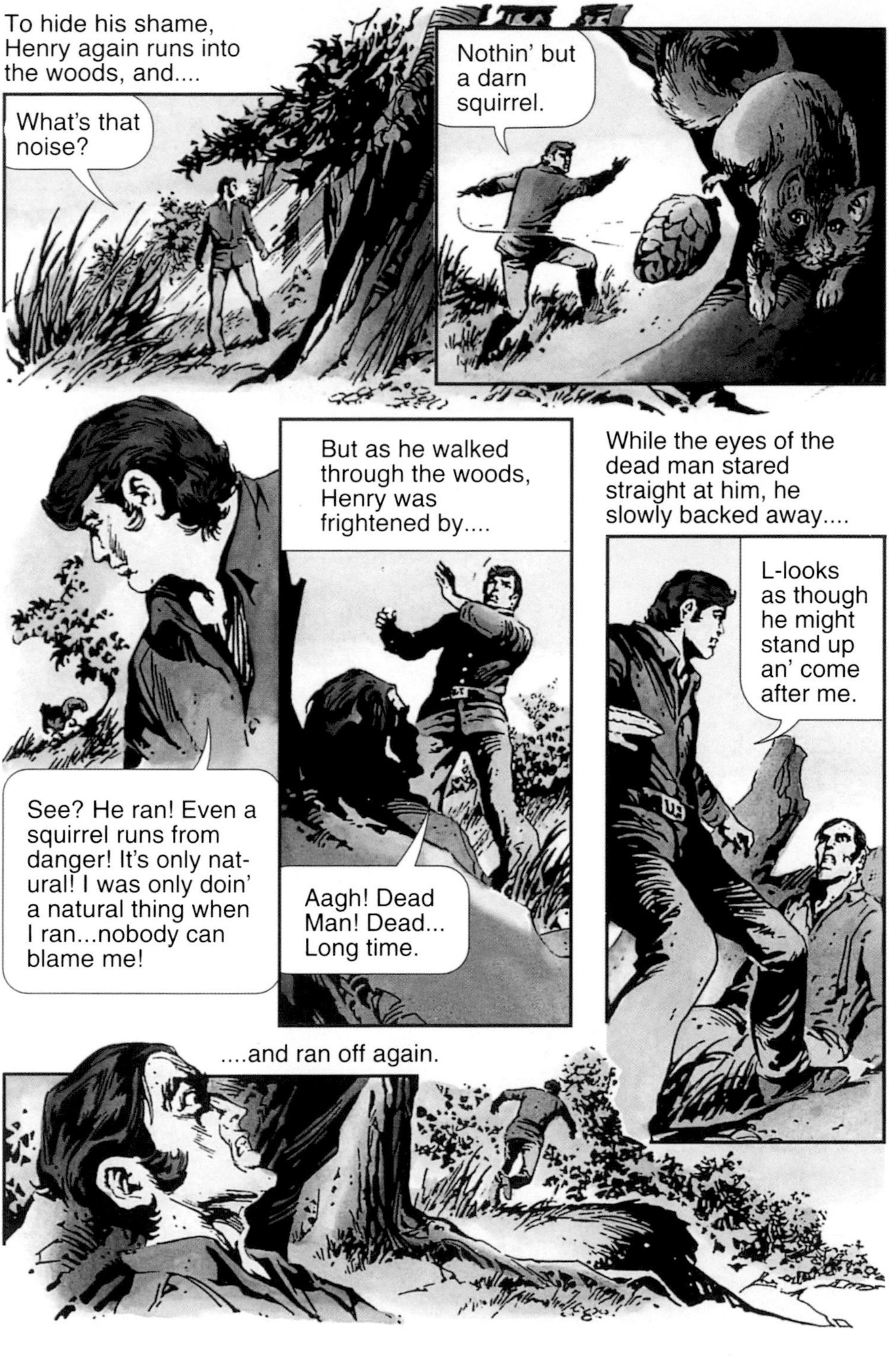

To hide his shame, Henry again runs into the woods, and....
What's that noise?
Nothin' but a darn squirrel.
See? He ran! Even a squirrel runs from danger! It's only natural! I was only doin' a natural thing when I ran...nobody can blame me!
But as he walked through the woods, Henry was frightened by....
Aagh! Dead Man! Dead... Long time.
While the eyes of the dead man stared straight at him, he slowly backed away....
L-looks as though he might stand up an' come after me.
....and ran off again.

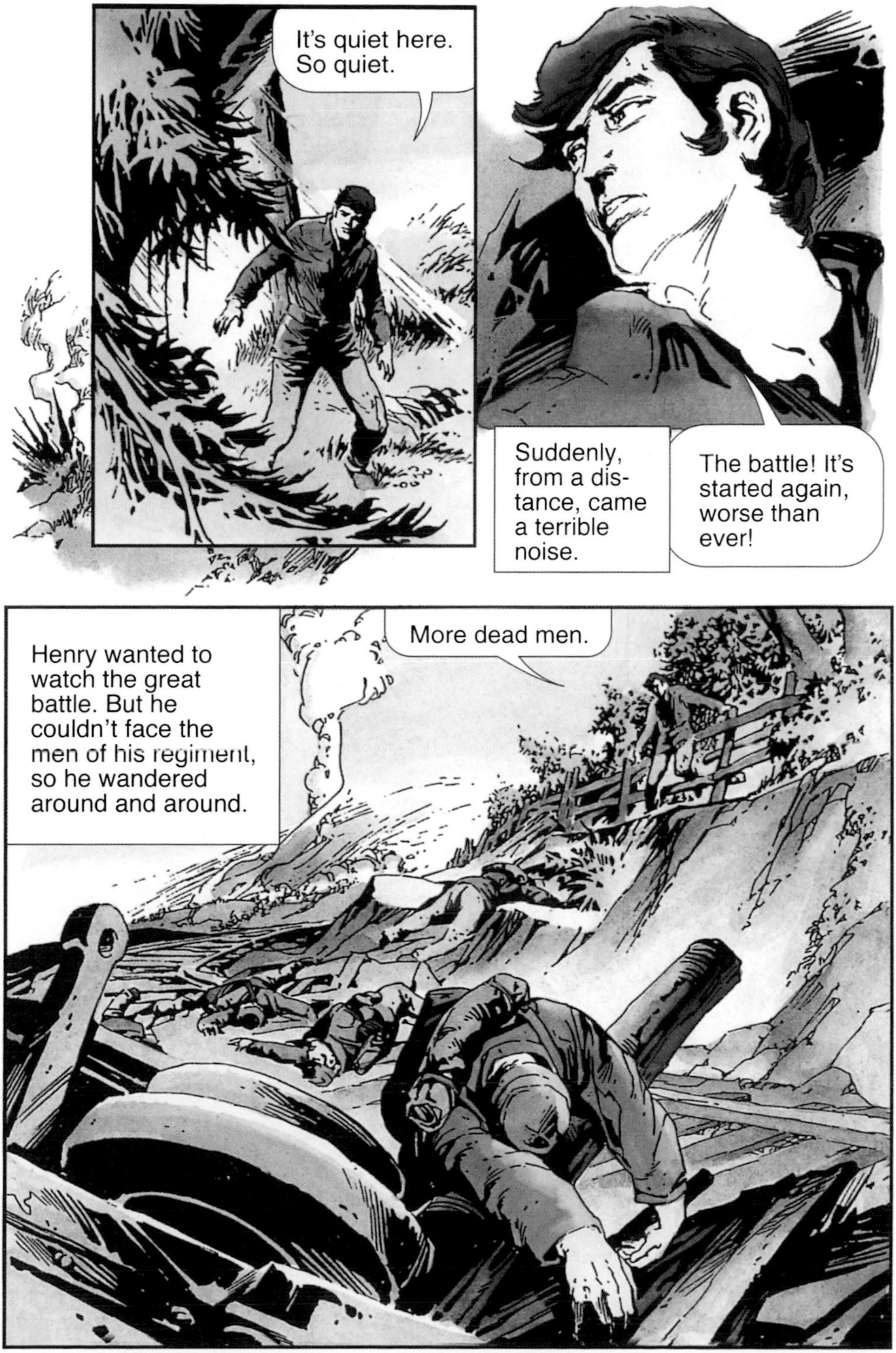
It's quiet here. So quiet.
Suddenly, from a distance, came a terrible noise.
The battle! It's started again, worse than ever!
Henry wanted to watch the great battle. But he couldn't face the men of his regiment, so he wandered around and around.
More dead men.

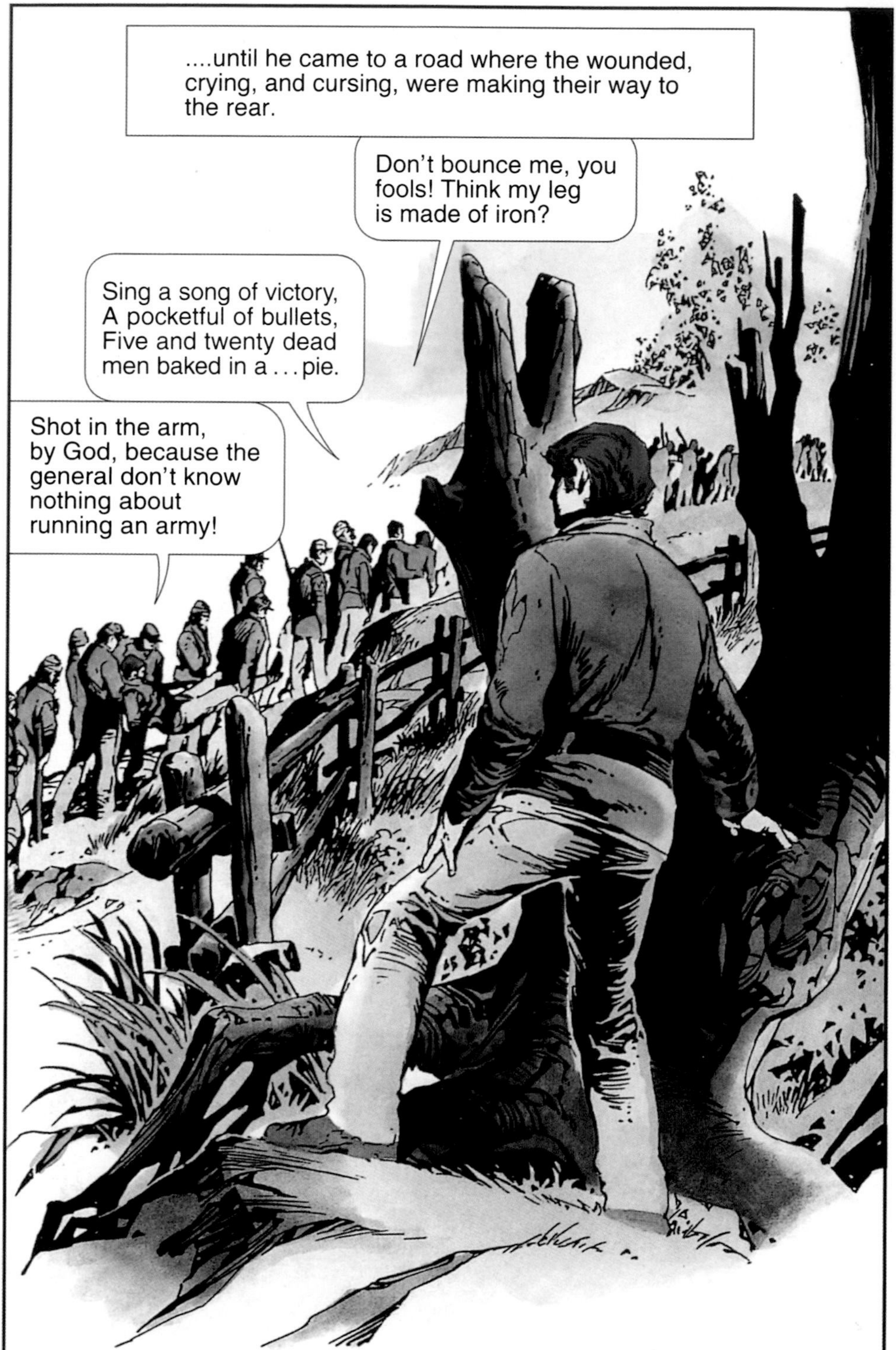
....until he came to a road where the wounded, crying, and cursing, were making their way to the rear.
Don't bounce me, you fools! Think my leg is made of iron?
Sing a song of victory, A pocketful of bullets, Five and twenty dead men baked in a . . . pie.
Shot in the arm, by God, because the general don't know nothing about running an army!

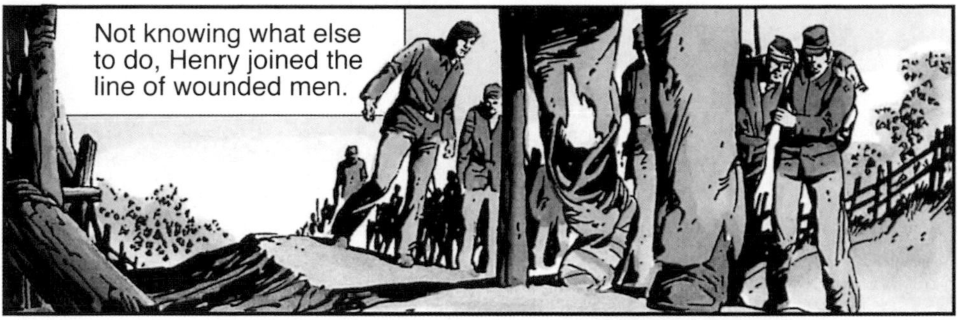
Not knowing what else to do, Henry joined the line of wounded men.

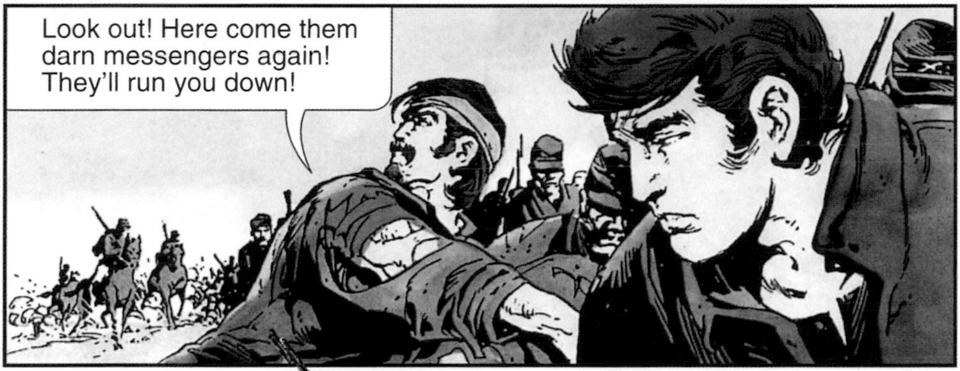
Look out! Here come them darn messengers again! They'll run you down!

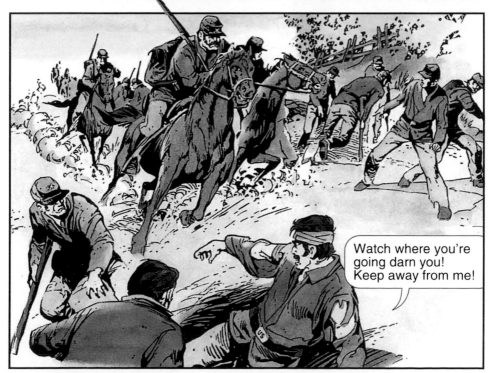

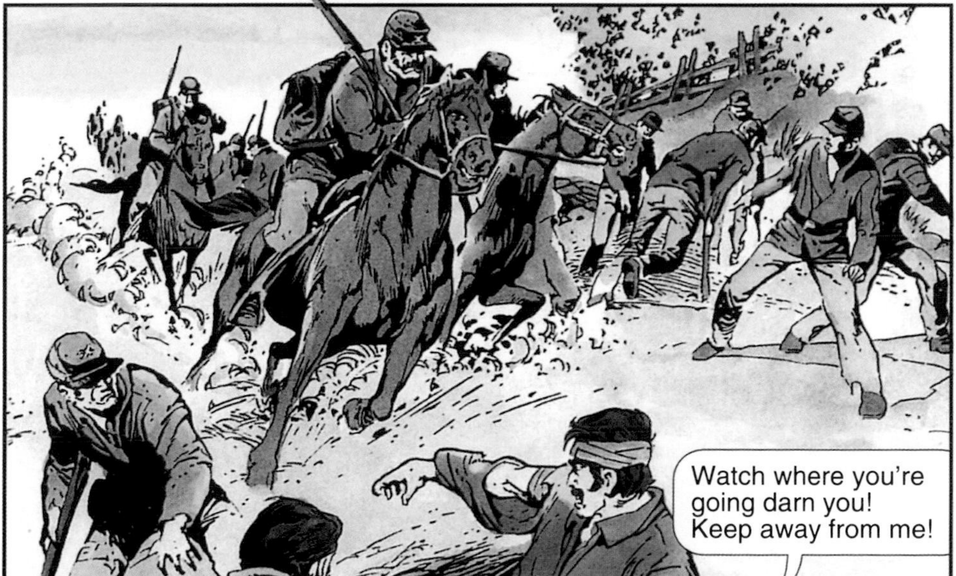
Watch where you're going darn you! Keep away from me!

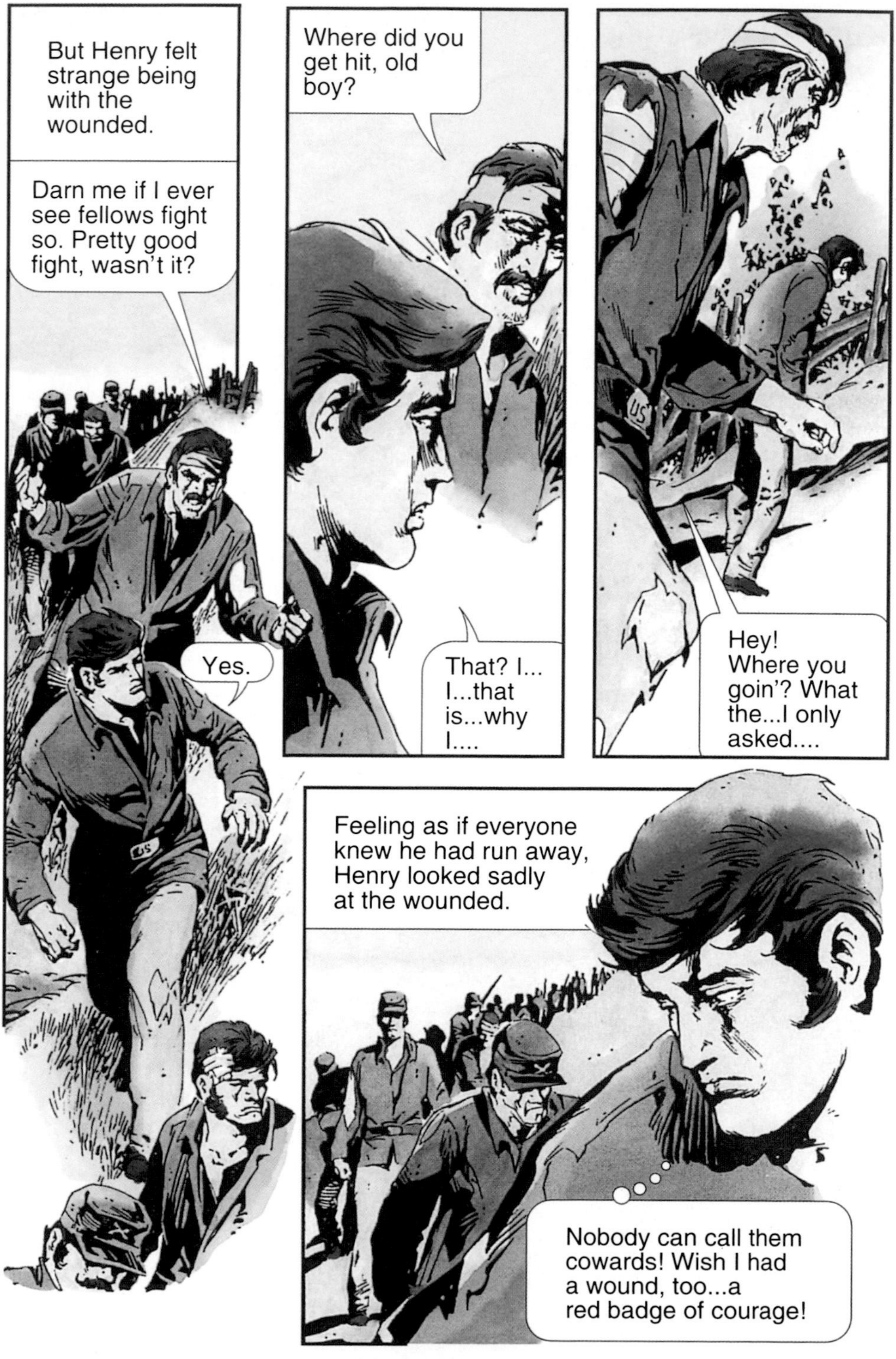
But Henry felt strange being with the wounded.
Darn me if I ever see fellows fight so. Pretty good fight, wasn't it?
Yes.
Where did you get hit, old boy?
That? I... I...that is...why I....
Hey! Where you goin'? What the...I only asked....
Feeling as if everyone knew he had run away, Henry looked sadly at the wounded.
Nobody can call them cowards! Wish I had a wound, too...a red badge of courage!

Suddenly, he saw someone he knew with the wounded.

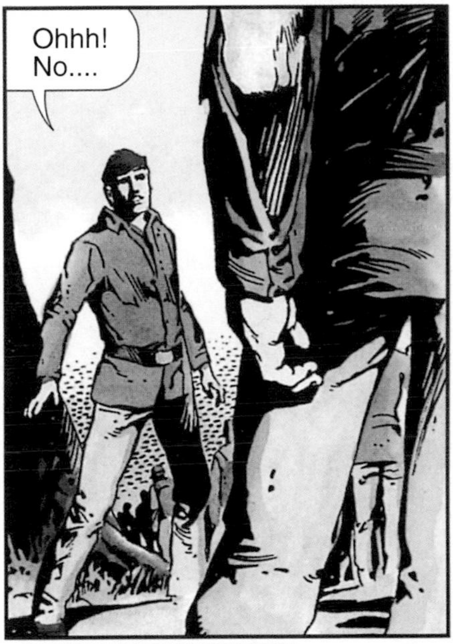
Ohhh!
No....

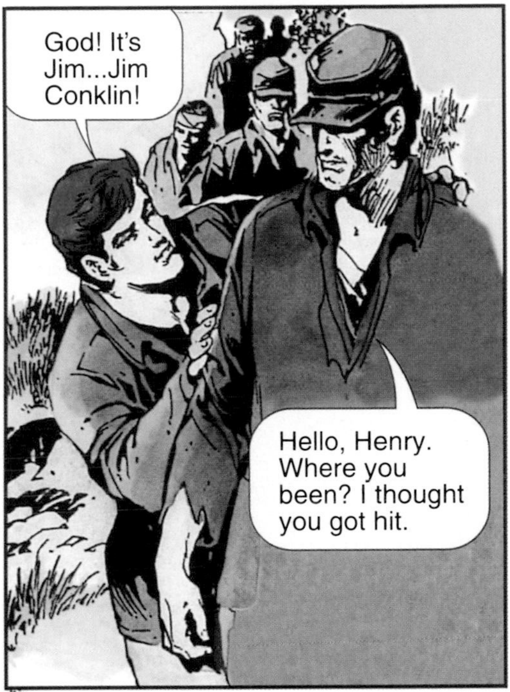
God! It's Jim...Jim Conklin!
Hello, Henry. Where you been? I thought you got hit.

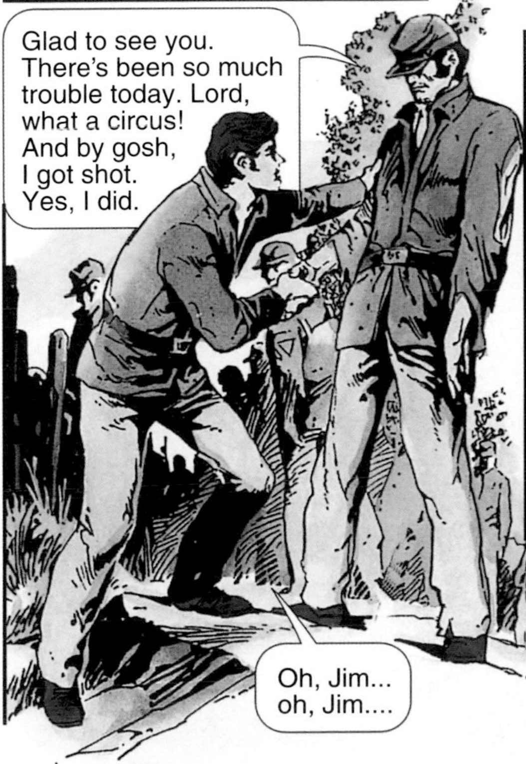
Glad to see you. There's been so much trouble today. Lord, what a circus! And by gosh, I got shot. Yes, I did.
Oh, Jim... oh, Jim....

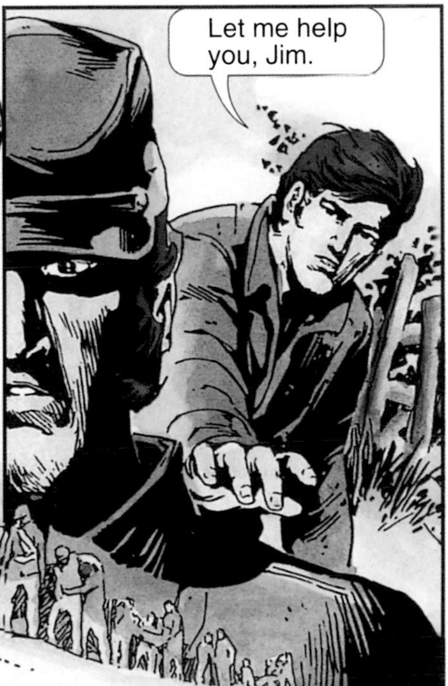
Let me help you, Jim.

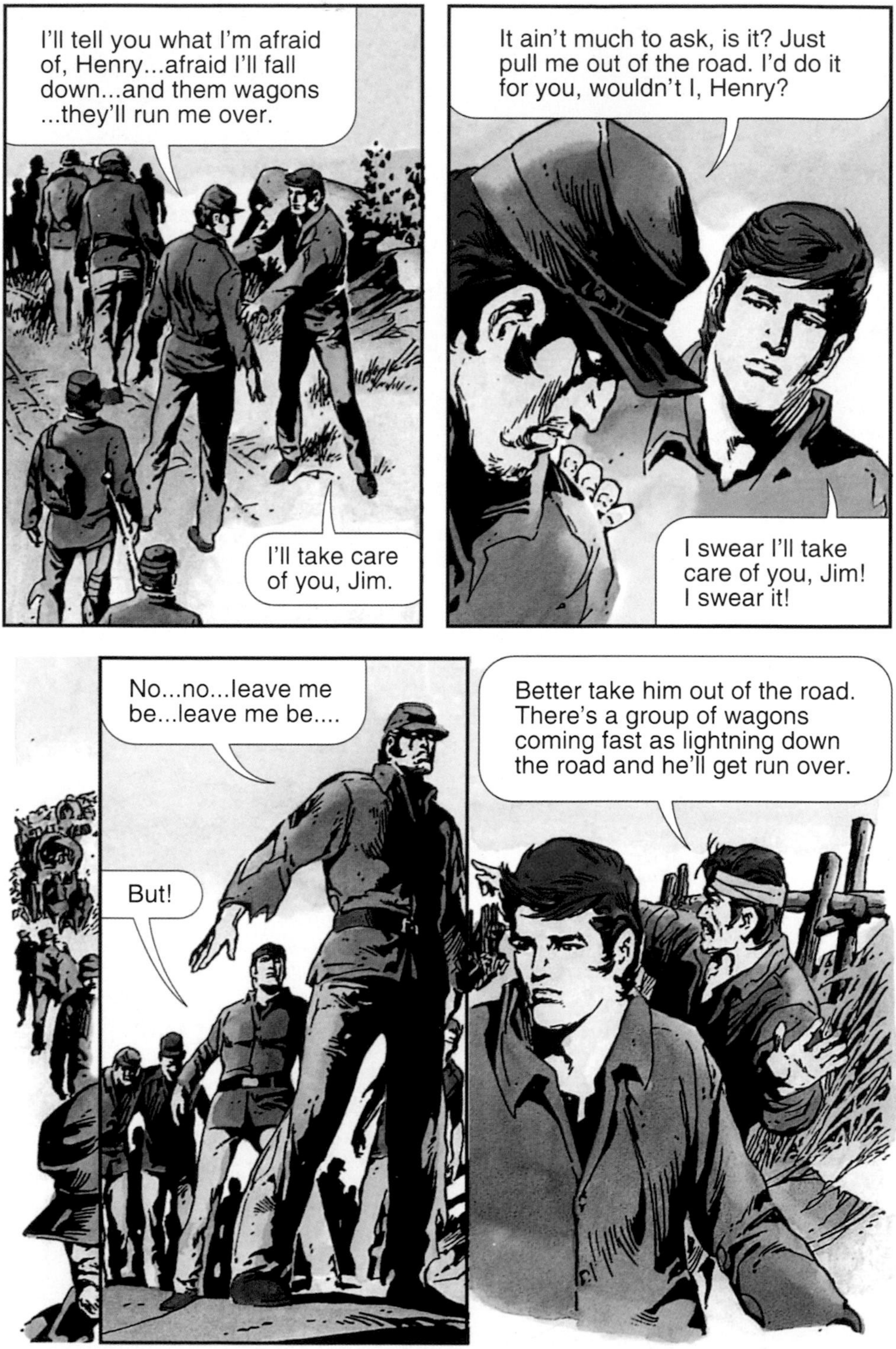
I'll tell you what I'm afraid of, Henry...afraid I'll fall down...and them wagons ...they'll run me over.
I'll take care of you, Jim.
It ain't much to ask, is it? Just pull me out of the road. I'd do it for you, wouldn't I, Henry?
I swear I'll take care of you, Jim! I swear it!
No...no...leave me be...leave me be....
But!
Better take him out of the road. There's a group of wagons coming fast as lightning down the road and he'll get run over.

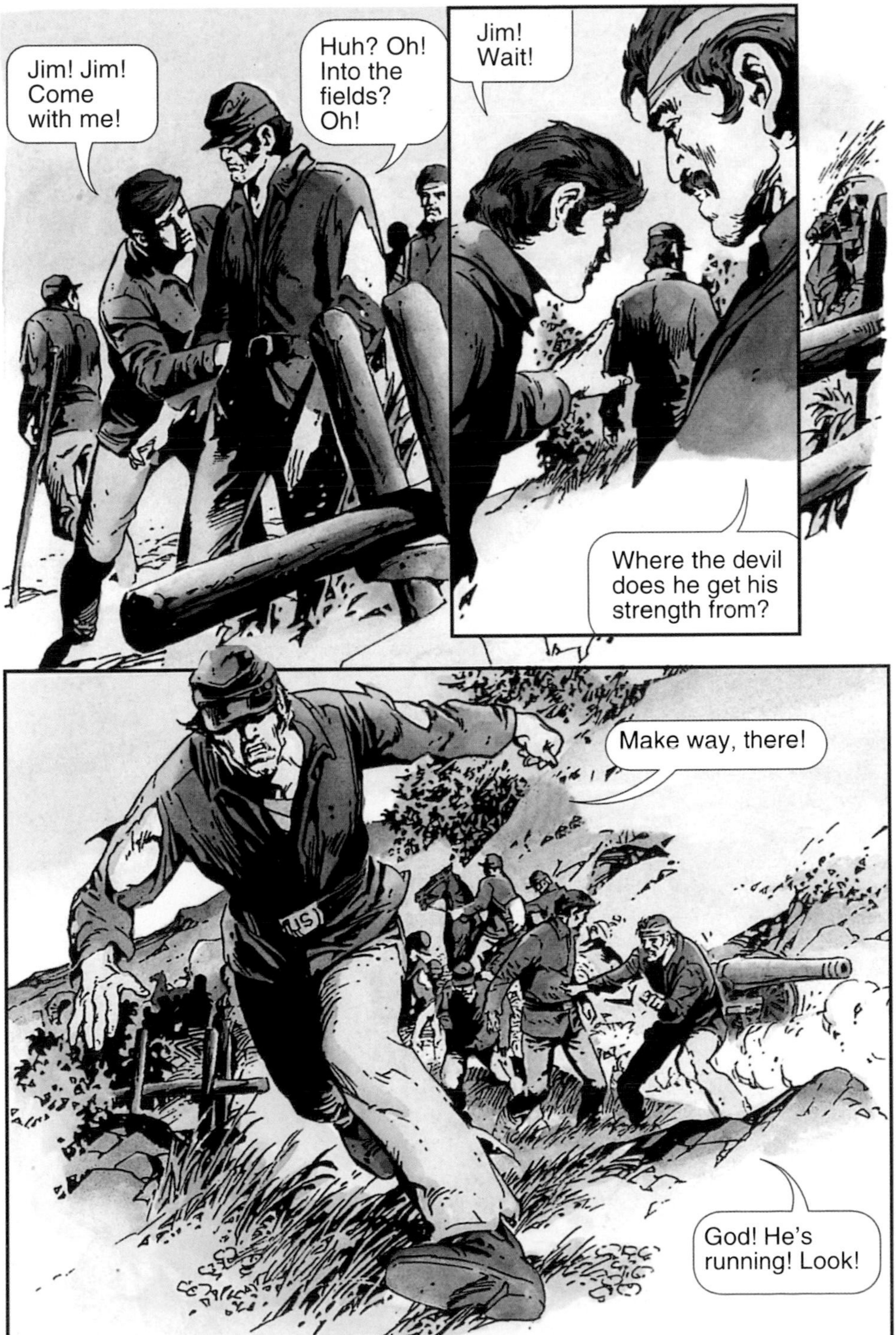
Jim! Jim! Come with me!
Huh? Oh! Into the fields? Oh!
Jim! Wait!
Where the devil does he get his strength from?
Make way, there!
God! He's running! Look!

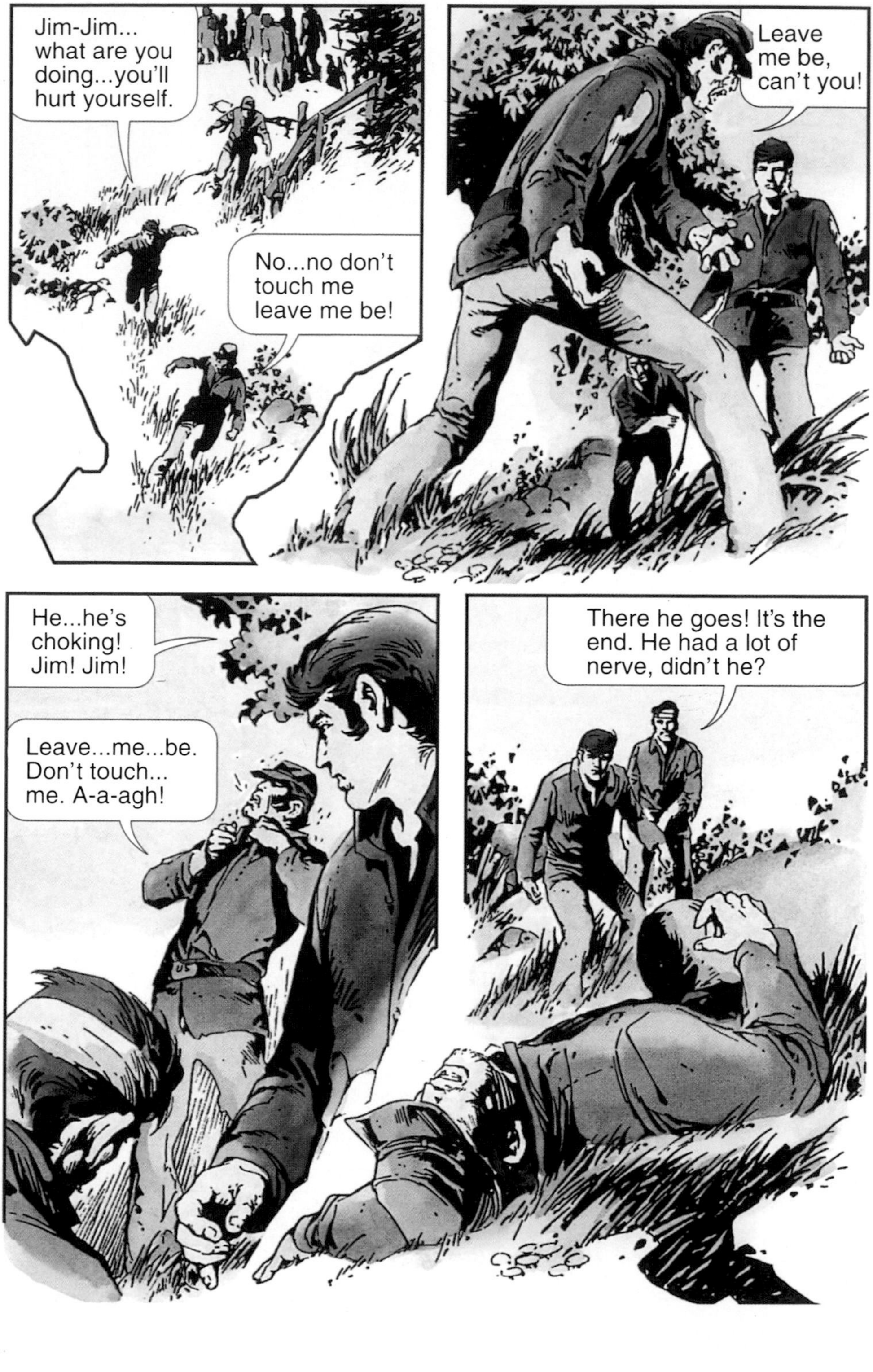
Jim-Jim... what are you doing...you'll hurt yourself.
No...no don't touch me leave me be!
Leave me be, can't you!
He...he's choking! Jim! Jim!
Leave...me...be. Don't touch... me. A-a-agh!
There he goes! It's the end. He had a lot of nerve, didn't he?

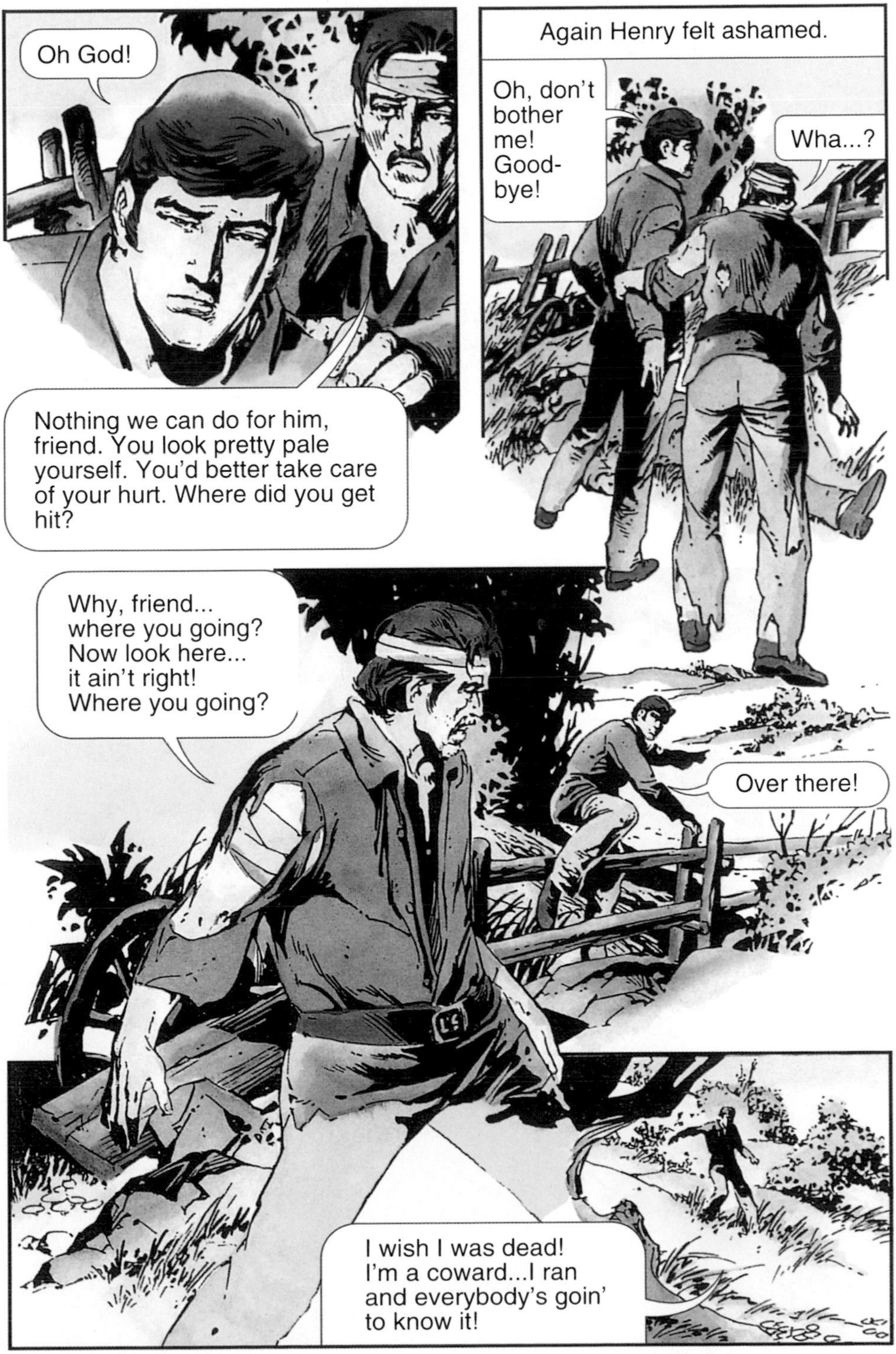
Oh God!
Nothing we can do for him, friend. You look pretty pale yourself. You'd better take care of your hurt. Where did you get hit?
Again Henry felt ashamed.
Oh, don't bother me! Good-bye!
Wha...?
Why, friend... where you going? Now look here... it ain't right! Where you going?
Over there!
I wish I was dead! I'm a coward...I ran and everybody's goin' to know it!

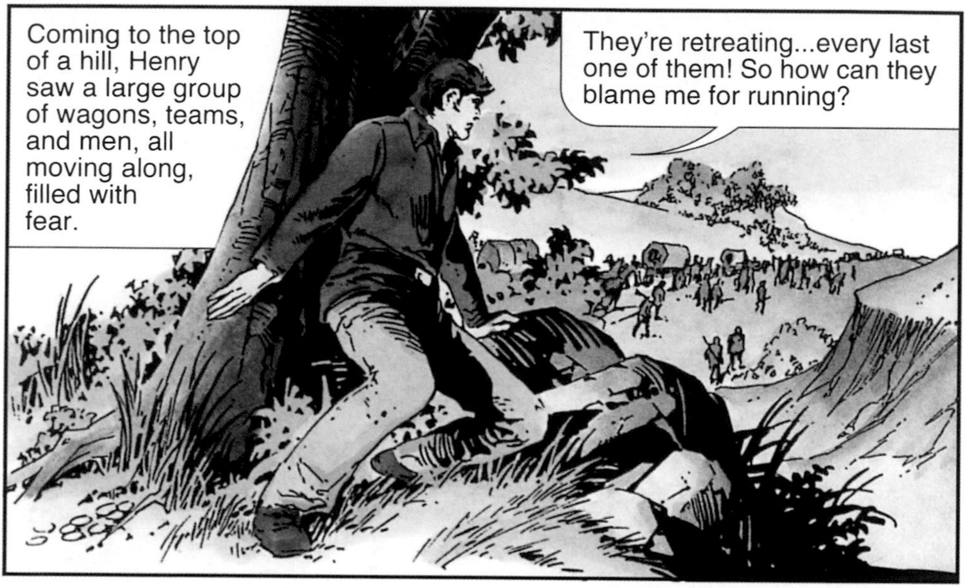
Coming to the top of a hill, Henry saw a large group of wagons, teams, and men, all moving along, filled with fear.
They're retreating...every last one of them! So how can they blame me for running?

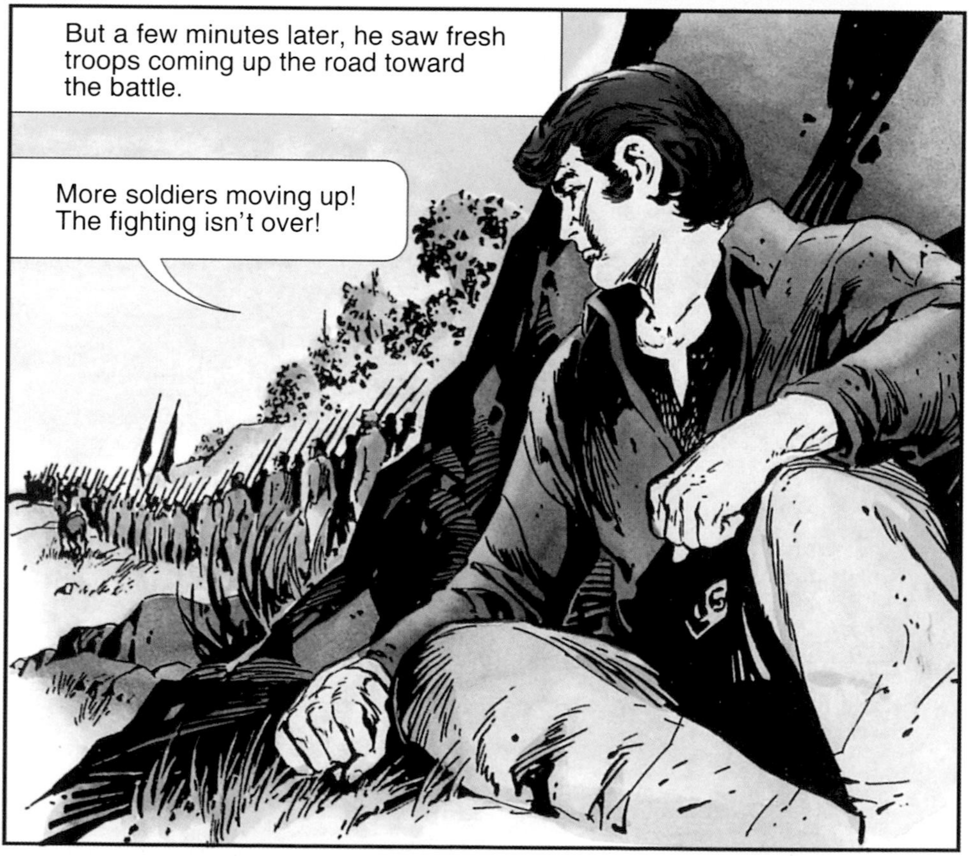
But a few minutes later, he saw fresh troops coming up the road toward the battle.
More soldiers moving up! The fighting isn't over!

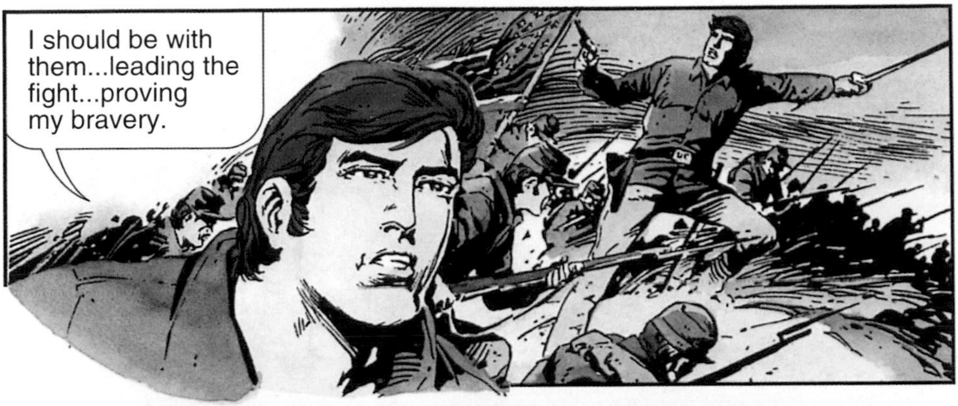
I should be with them...leading the fight...proving my bravery.

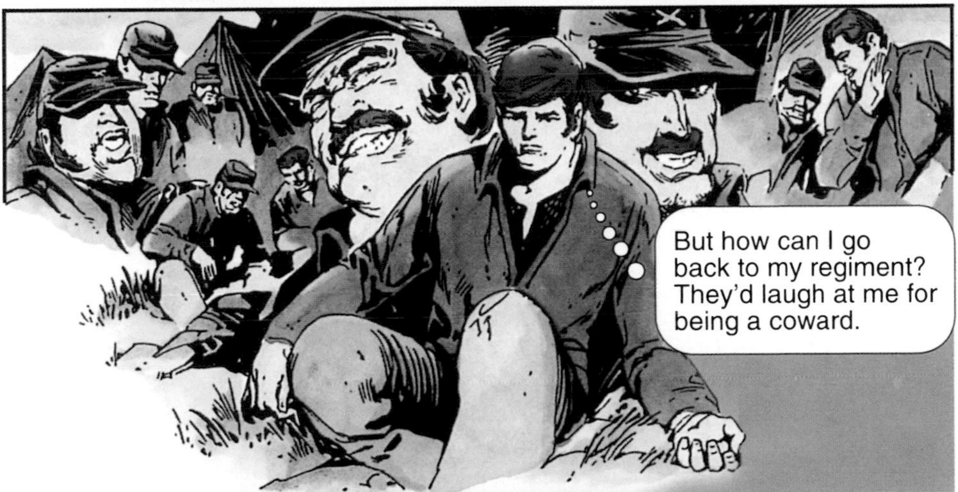
But how can I go back to my regiment? They'd laugh at me for being a coward.

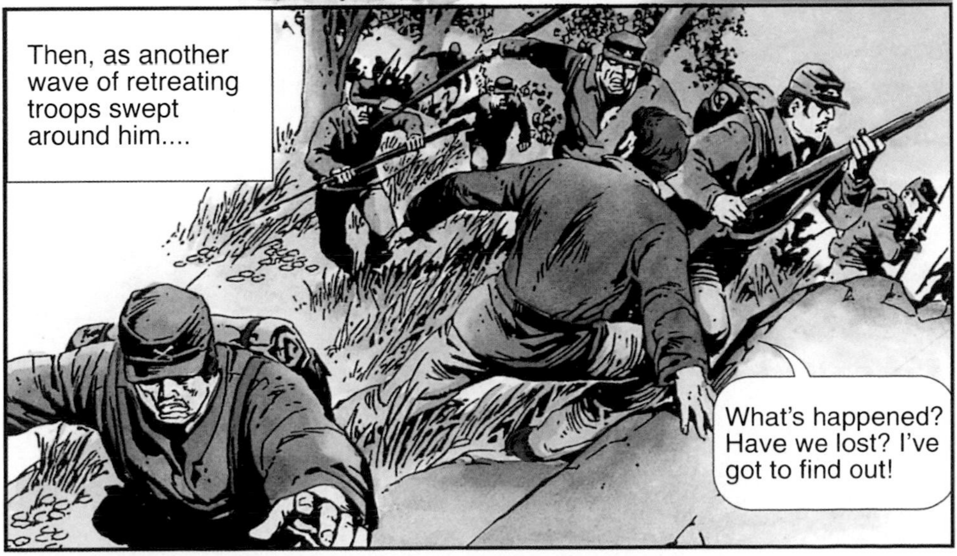
Then, as another wave of retreating troops swept around him....
What's happened? Have we lost? I've got to find out!

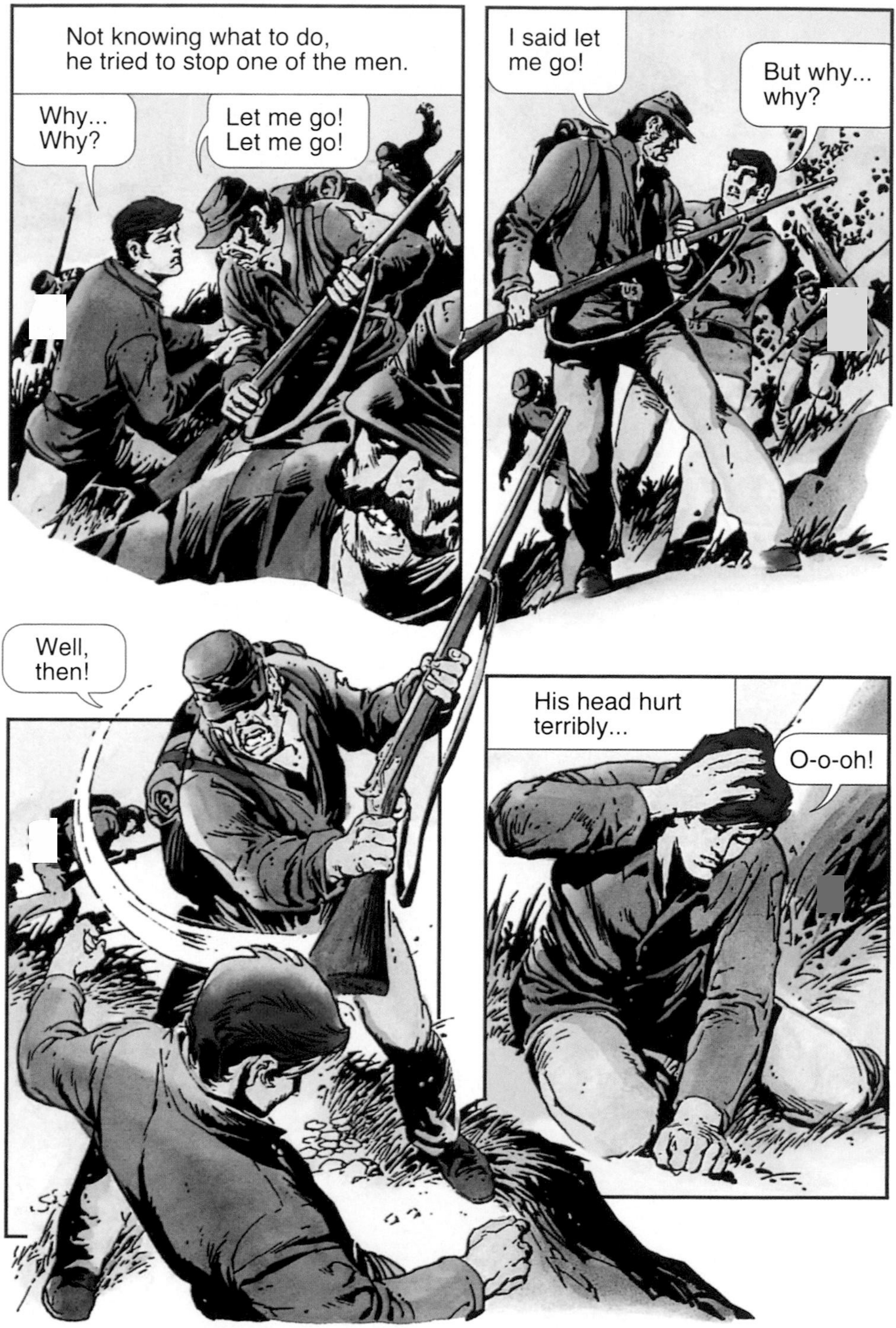
Not knowing what to do,
he tried to stop one of the men.
Why...
Why?
Let me go!
Let me go!
I said let
me go!
But why...
why?
Well,
then!
His head hurt
terribly...
O-o-oh!

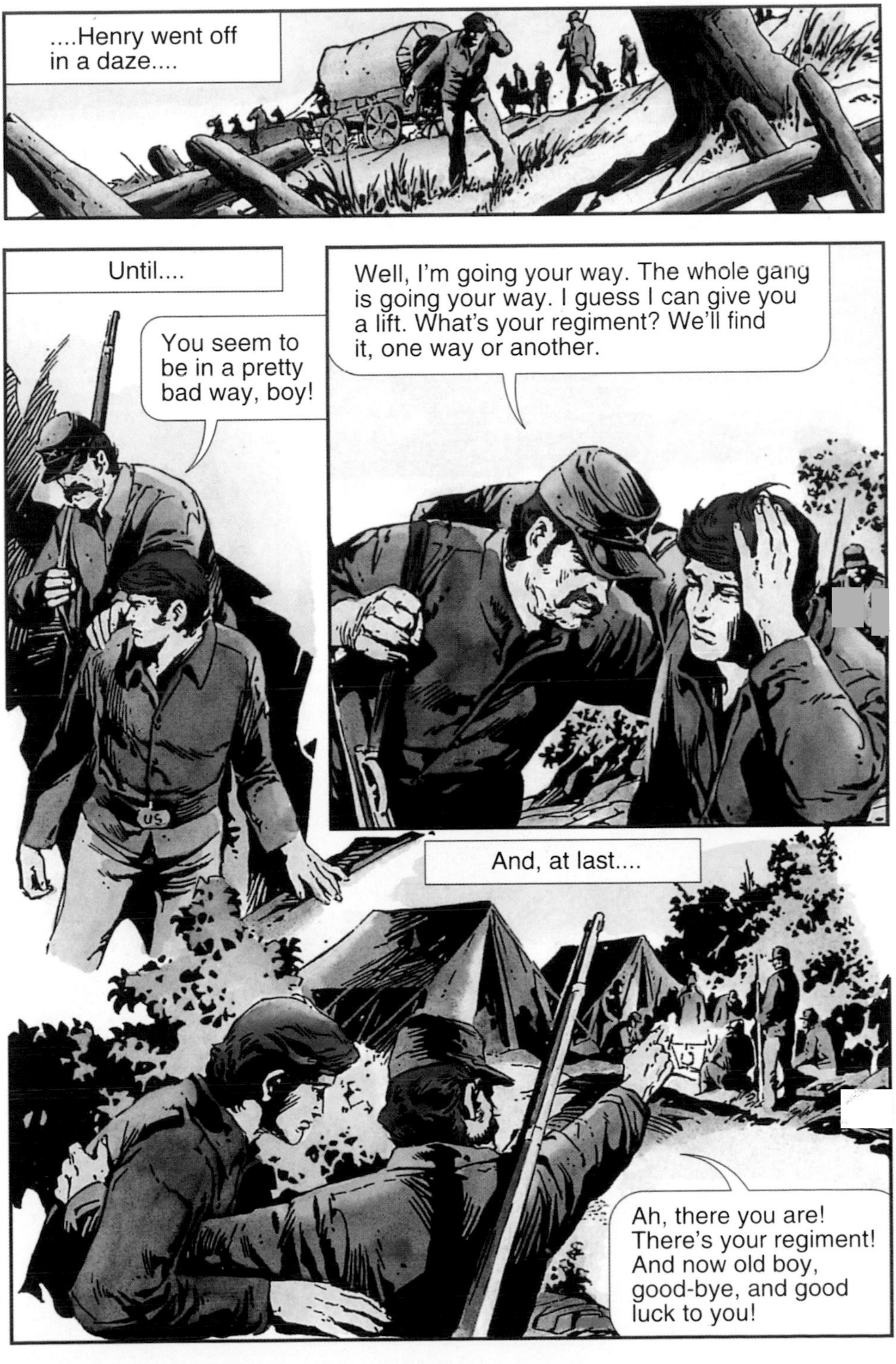
....Henry went off in a daze....
Until....
You seem to be in a pretty bad way, boy!
Well, I'm going your way. The whole gang is going your way. I guess I can give you a lift. What's your regiment? We'll find it, one way or another.
And, at last....
Ah, there you are! There's your regiment! And now old boy, good-bye, and good luck to you!

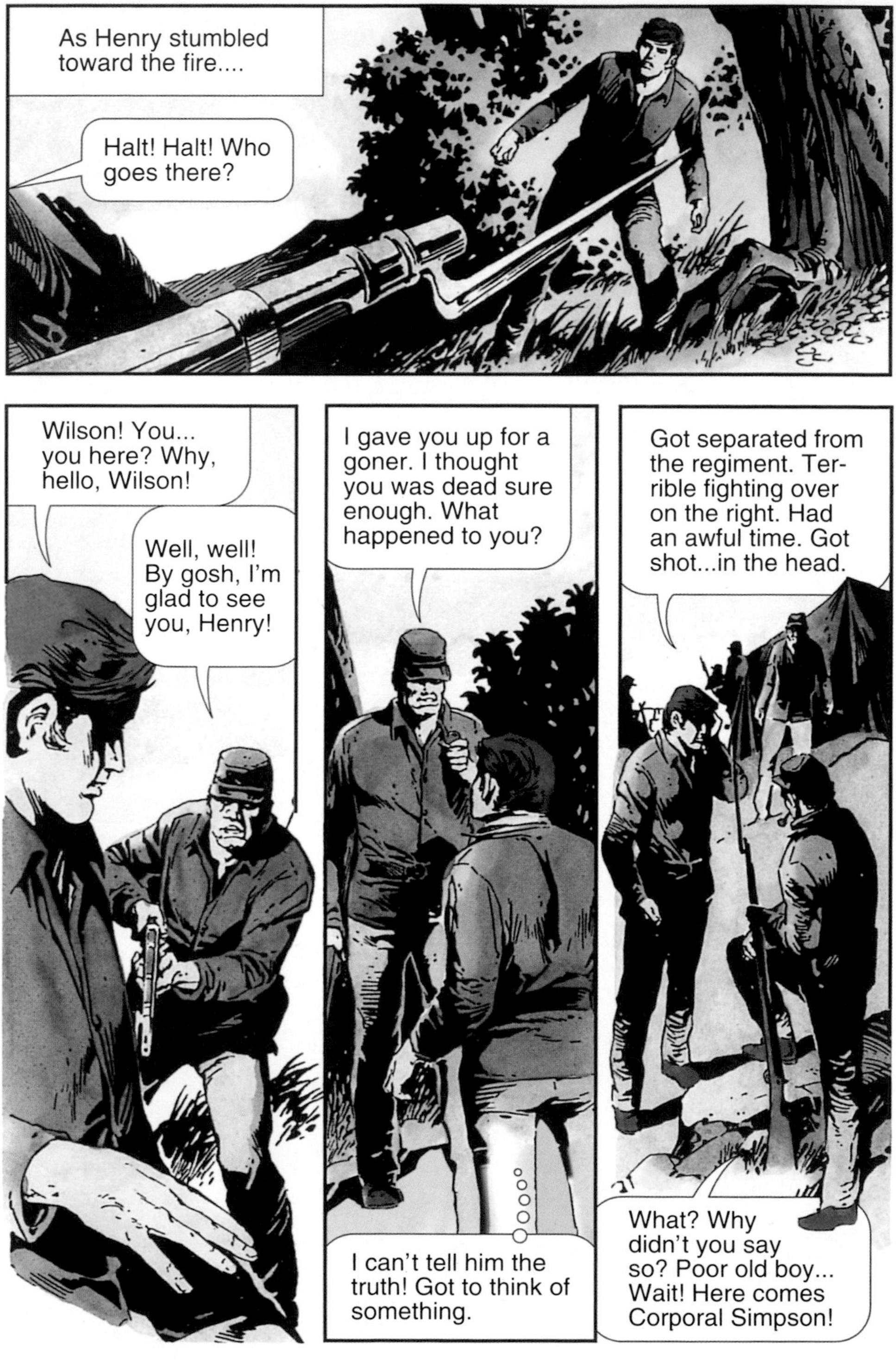
As Henry stumbled toward the fire....
Halt! Halt! Who goes there?
Wilson! You... you here? Why, hello, Wilson!
Well, well! By gosh, I'm glad to see you, Henry!
I gave you up for a goner. I thought you was dead sure enough. What happened to you?
I can't tell him the truth! Got to think of something.
Got separated from the regiment. Terrible fighting over on the right. Had an awful time. Got shot...in the head.
What? Why didn't you say so? Poor old boy... Wait! Here comes Corporal Simpson!

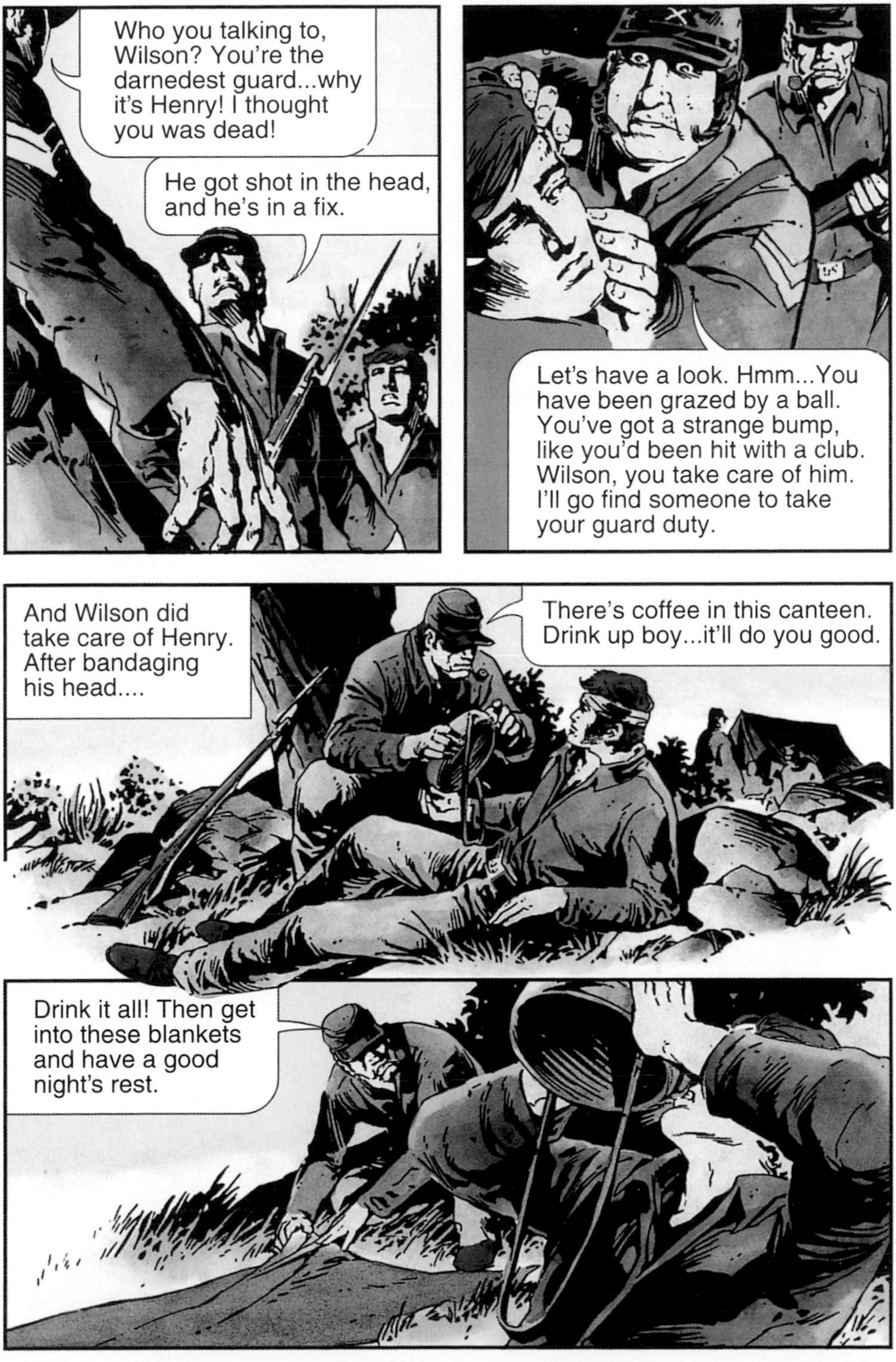
Who you talking to, Wilson? You're the darnedest guard...why it's Henry! I thought you was dead!
He got shot in the head, and he's in a fix.
Let's have a look. Hmm...You have been grazed by a ball. You've got a strange bump, like you'd been hit with a club. Wilson, you take care of him. I'll go find someone to take your guard duty.
And Wilson did take care of Henry. After bandaging his head....
There's coffee in this canteen. Drink up boy...it'll do you good.
Drink it all! Then get into these blankets and have a good night's rest.

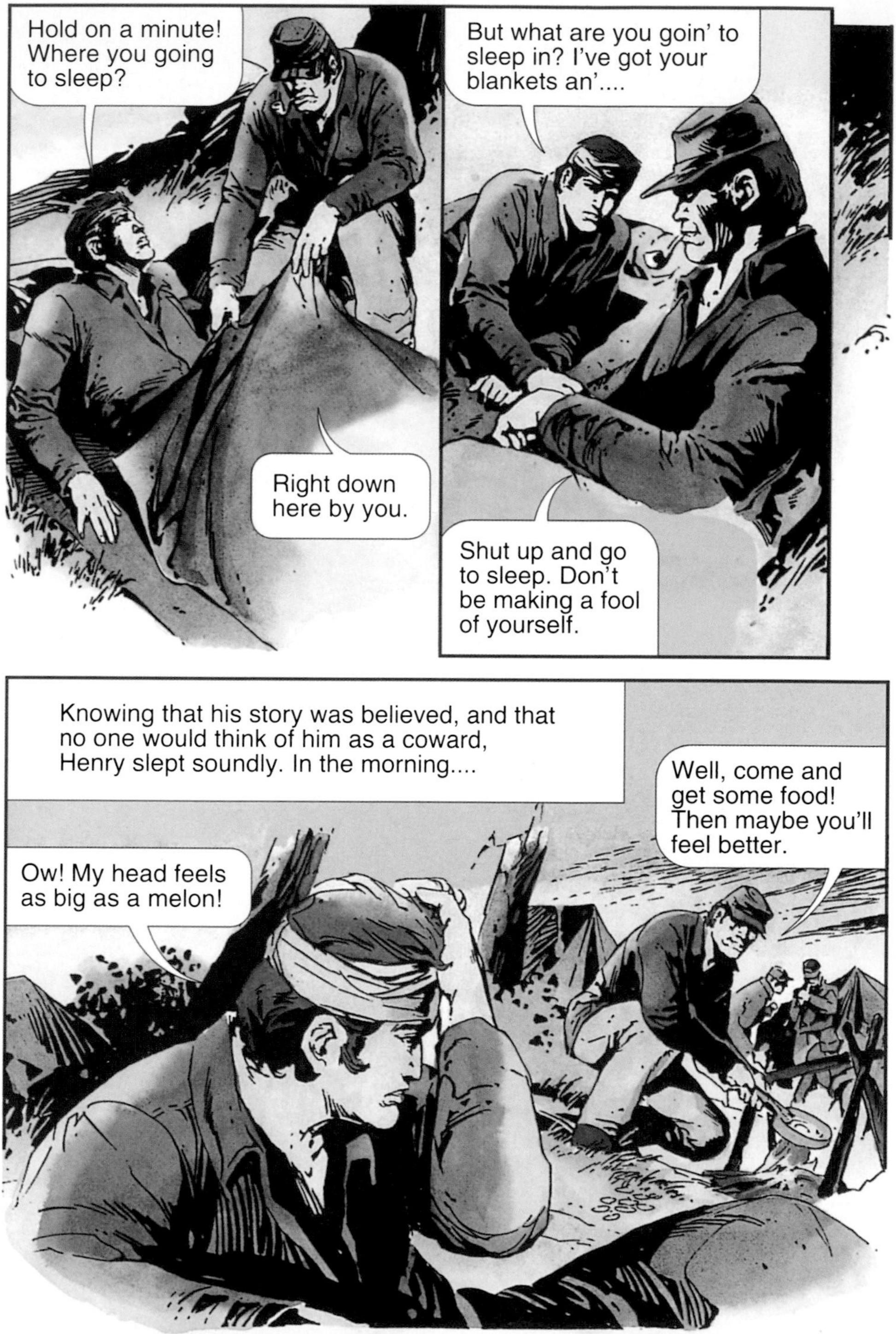
Hold on a minute! Where you going to sleep?
Right down here by you.
But what are you goin' to sleep in? I've got your blankets an'....
Shut up and go to sleep. Don't be making a fool of yourself.
Knowing that his story was believed, and that no one would think of him as a coward, Henry slept soundly. In the morning....
Ow! My head feels as big as a melon!
Well, come and get some food! Then maybe you'll feel better.

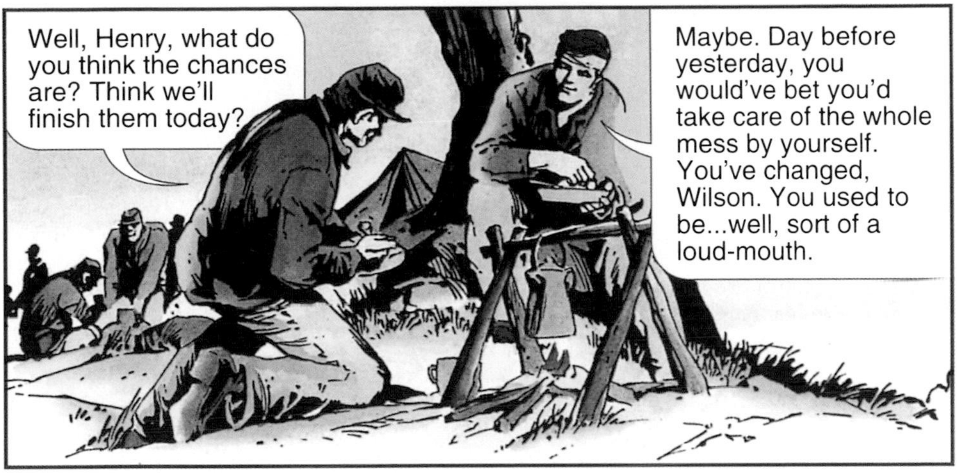
Well, Henry, what do you think the chances are? Think we'll finish them today?
Maybe. Day before yesterday, you would've bet you'd take care of the whole mess by yourself. You've changed, Wilson. You used to be...well, sort of a loud-mouth.

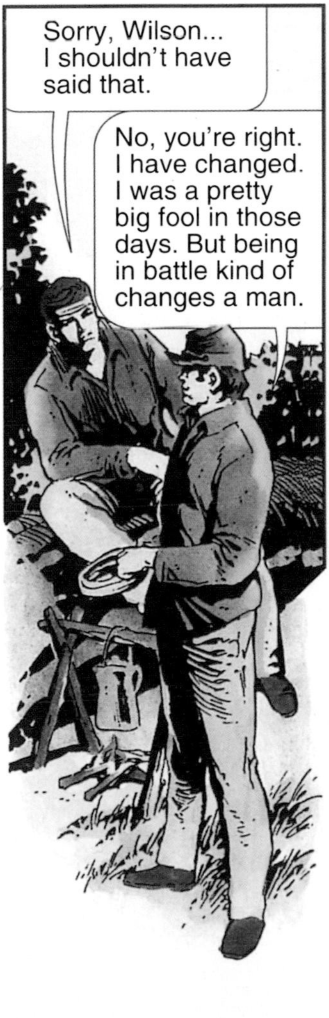
Sorry, Wilson... I shouldn't have said that.
No, you're right. I have changed. I was a pretty big fool in those days. But being in battle kind of changes a man.

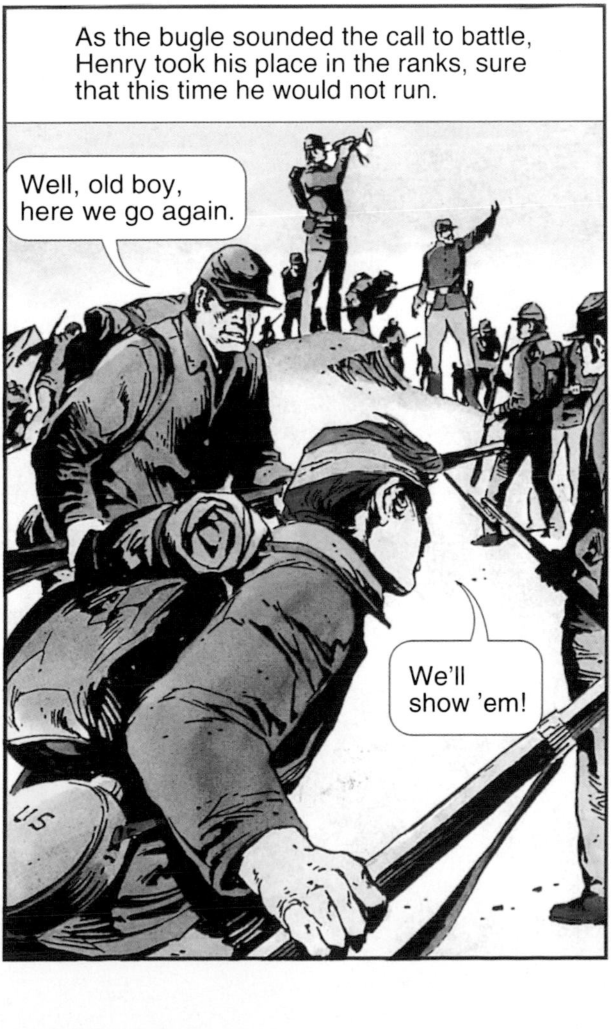
As the bugle sounded the call to battle, Henry took his place in the ranks, sure that this time he would not run.
Well, old boy, here we go again.
We'll show 'em!
US

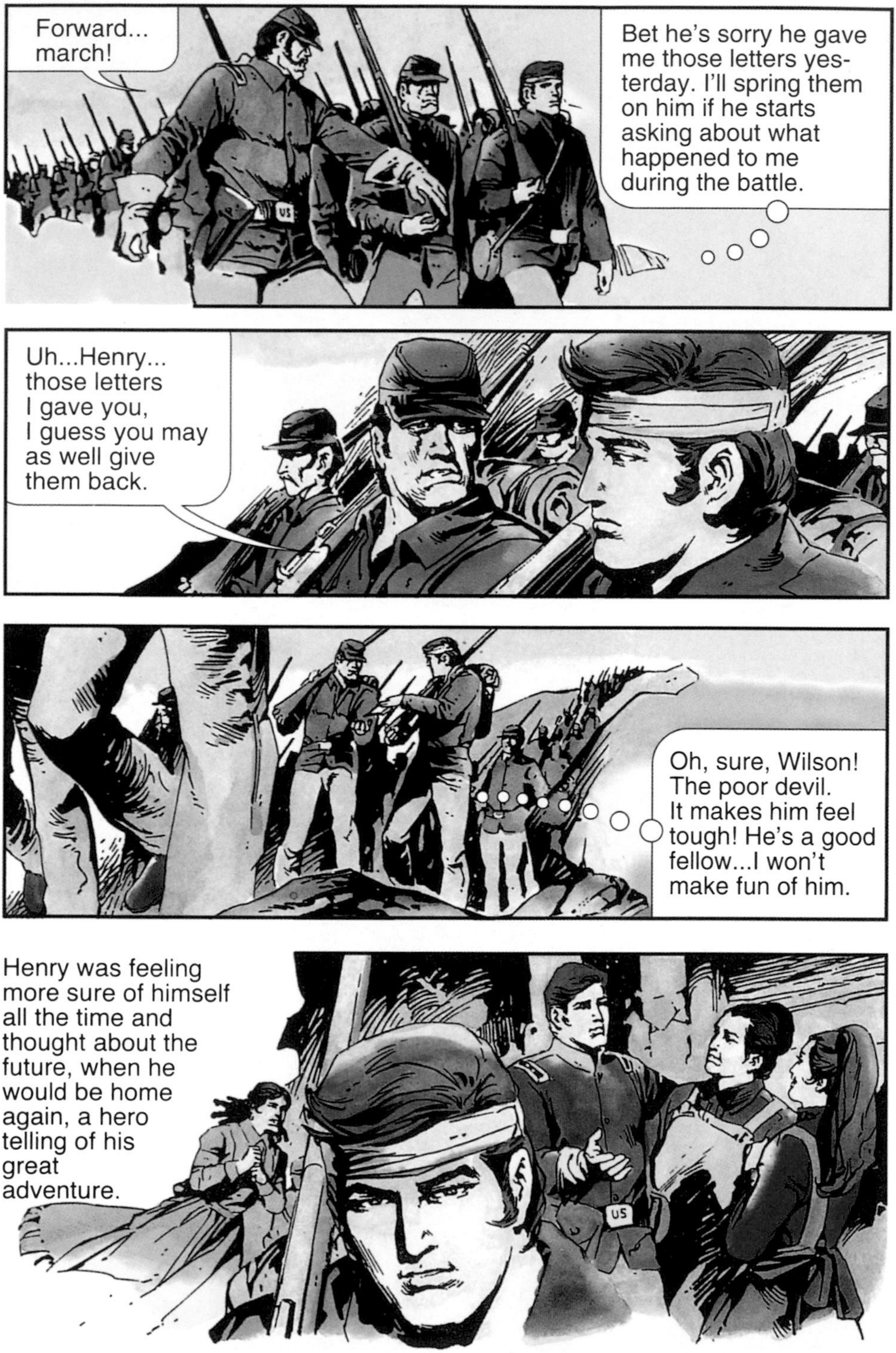
Forward... march!
Bet he's sorry he gave me those letters yesterday. I'll spring them on him if he starts asking about what happened to me during the battle.
Uh...Henry... those letters I gave you, I guess you may as well give them back.
Oh, sure, Wilson! The poor devil. It makes him feel tough! He's a good fellow...I won't make fun of him.
Henry was feeling more sure of himself all the time and thought about the future, when he would be home again, a hero telling of his great adventure.

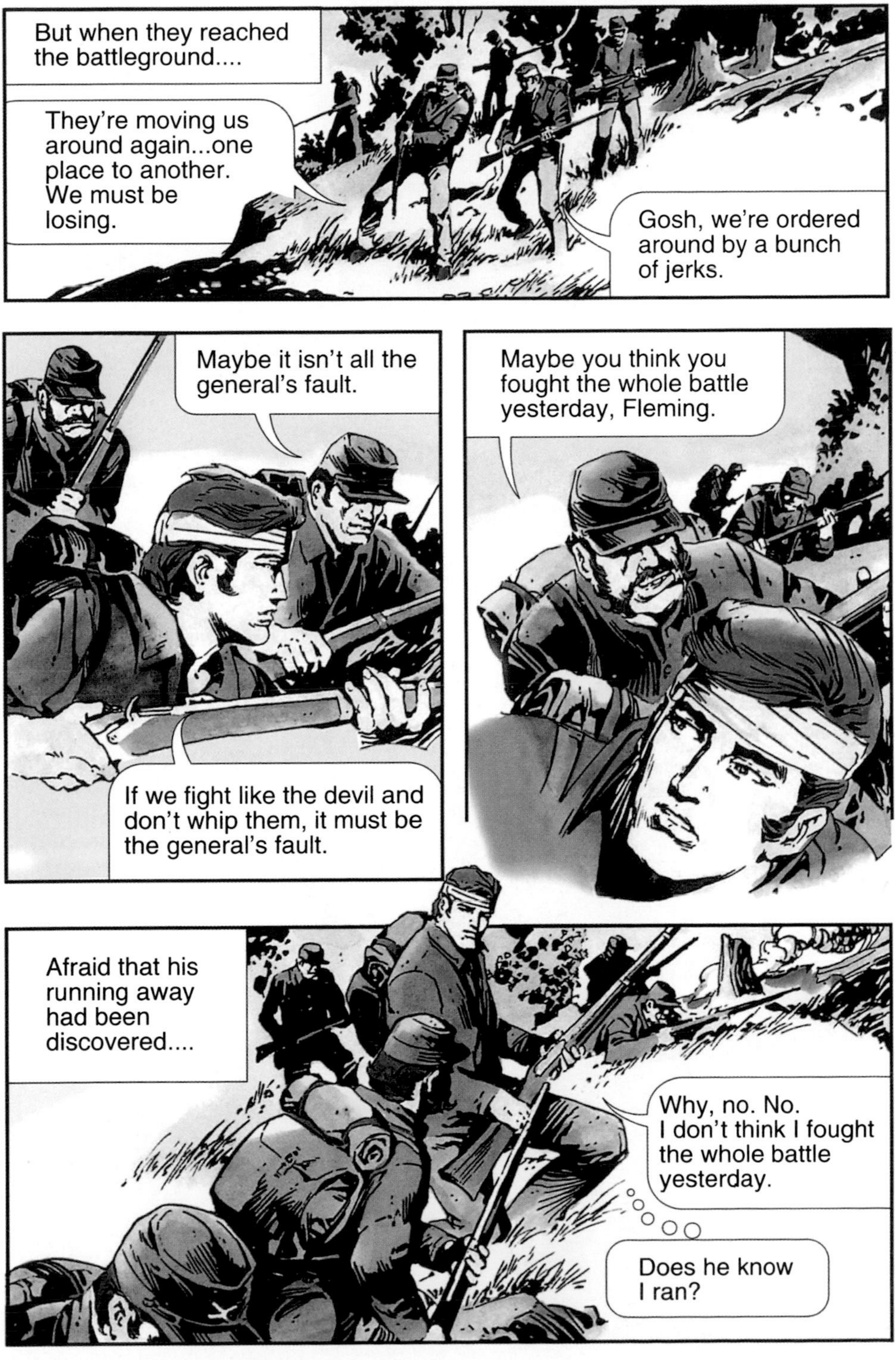
But when they reached the battleground....
They're moving us around again...one place to another. We must be losing.
Gosh, we're ordered around by a bunch of jerks.
Maybe it isn't all the general's fault.
If we fight like the devil and don't whip them, it must be the general's fault.
Maybe you think you fought the whole battle yesterday, Fleming.
Afraid that his running away had been discovered....
Why, no. No. I don't think I fought the whole battle yesterday.
Does he know I ran?

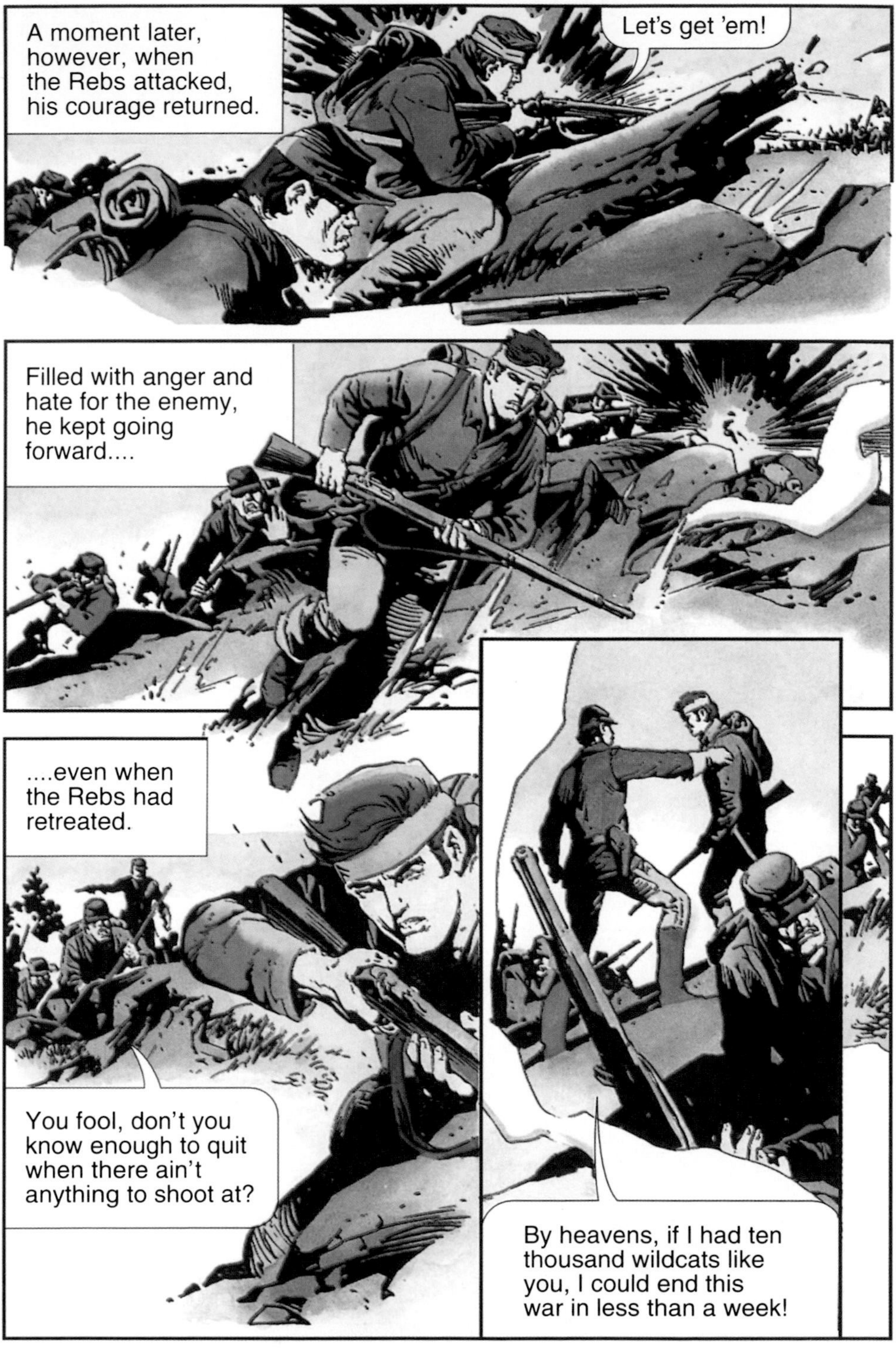

A moment later, however, when the Rebs attacked, his courage returned.
Let's get 'em!
Filled with anger and hate for the enemy, he kept going forward....
....even when the Rebs had retreated.
You fool, don't you know enough to quit when there ain't anything to shoot at?
By heavens, if I had ten thousand wildcats like you, I could end this war in less than a week!

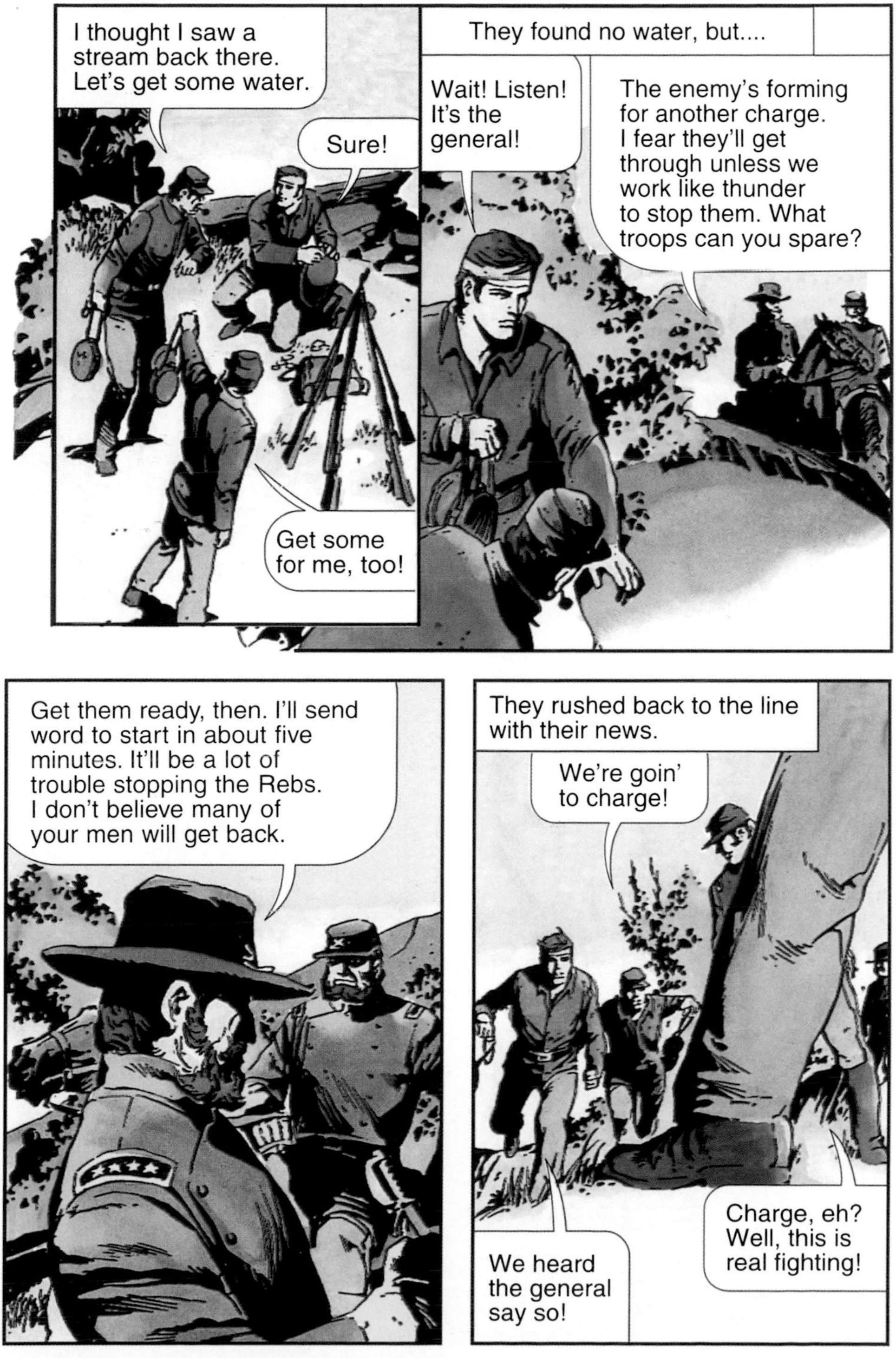
I thought I saw a stream back there. Let's get some water.
Sure!
Get some for me, too!
They found no water, but....
Wait! Listen! It's the general!
The enemy's forming for another charge. I fear they'll get through unless we work like thunder to stop them. What troops can you spare?
Get them ready, then. I'll send word to start in about five minutes. It'll be a lot of trouble stopping the Rebs. I don't believe many of your men will get back.
They rushed back to the line with their news.
We're goin' to charge!
We heard the general say so!
Charge, eh? Well, this is real fighting!

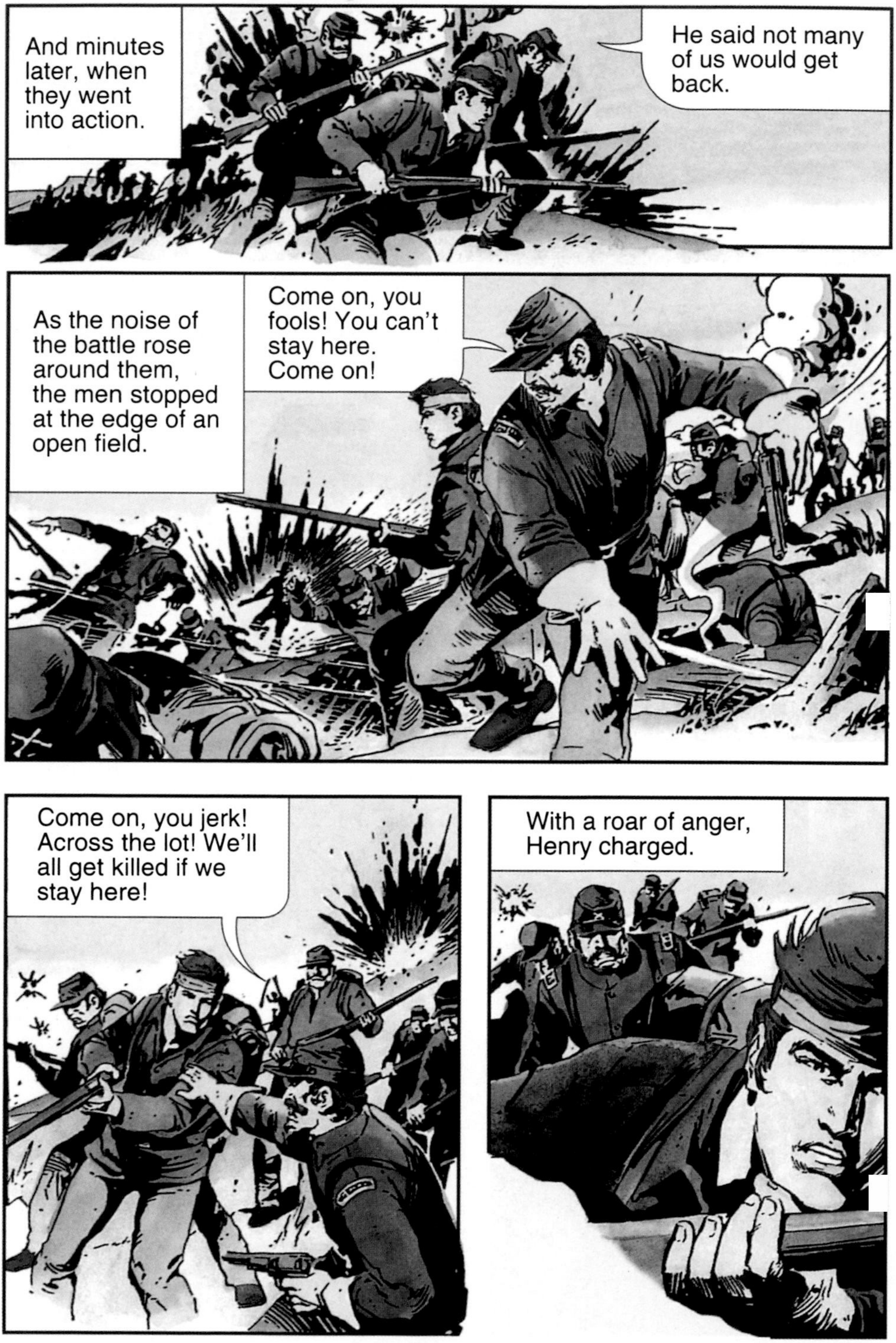
And minutes later, when they went into action.
He said not many of us would get back.
As the noise of the battle rose around them, the men stopped at the edge of an open field.
Come on, you fools! You can't stay here. Come on!
Come on, you jerk! Across the lot! We'll all get killed if we stay here!
With a roar of anger, Henry charged.

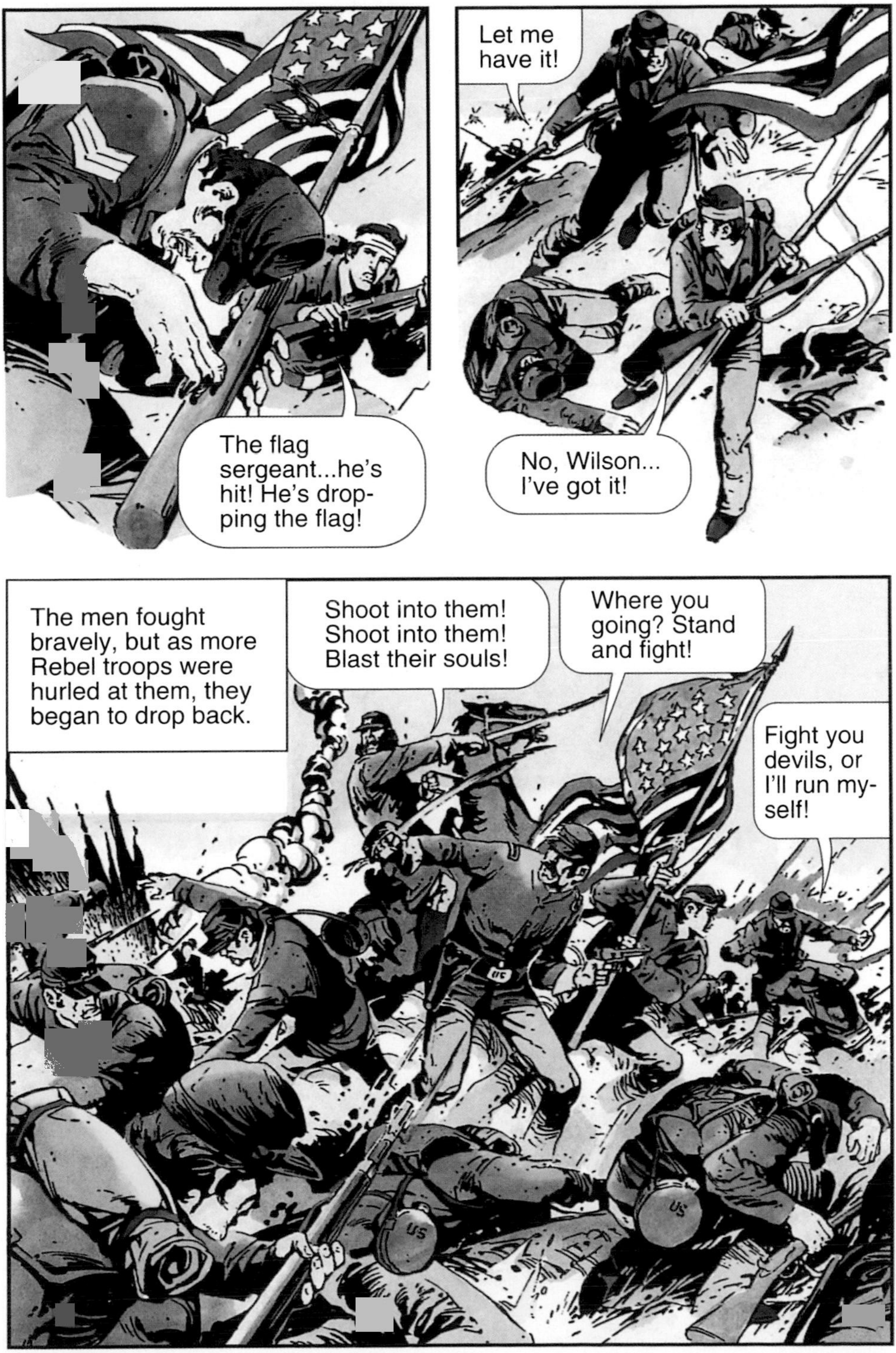
The flag sergeant...he's hit! He's dropping the flag!
Let me have it!
No, Wilson... I've got it!
The men fought bravely, but as more Rebel troops were hurled at them, they began to drop back.
Shoot into them! Shoot into them! Blast their souls!
Where you going? Stand and fight!
Fight you devils, or I'll run myself!

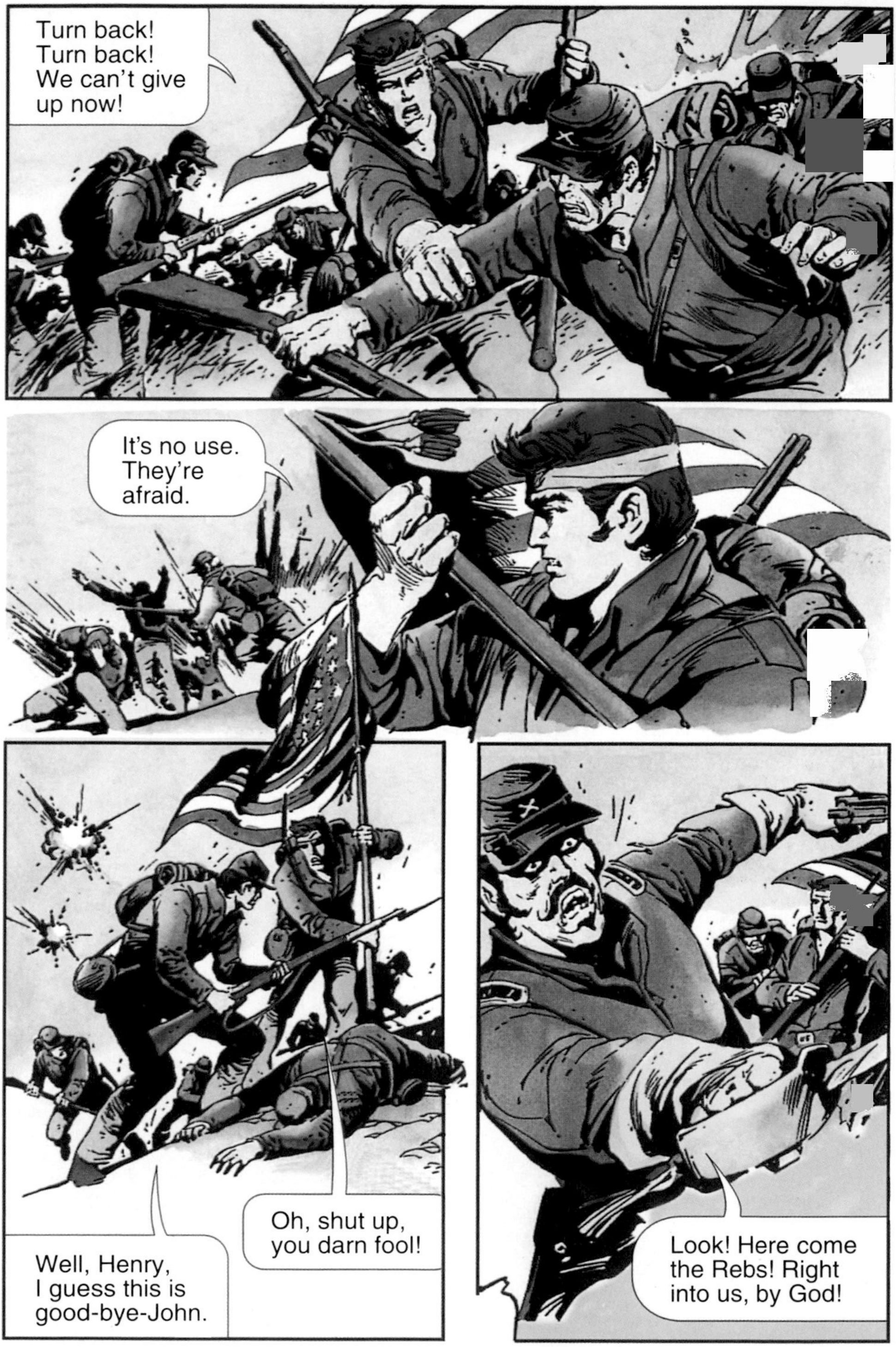
Turn back! Turn back! We can't give up now!
It's no use. They're afraid.
Well, Henry, I guess this is good-bye-John.
Oh, shut up, you darn fool!
Look! Here come the Rebs! Right into us, by God!

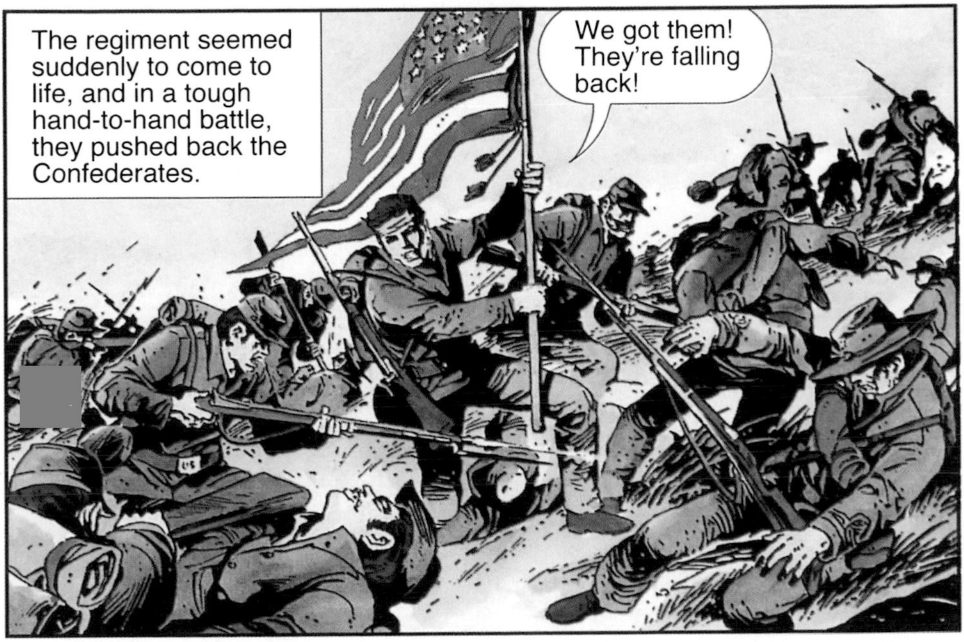
The regiment seemed suddenly to come to life, and in a tough hand-to-hand battle, they pushed back the Confederates.
We got them! They're falling back!

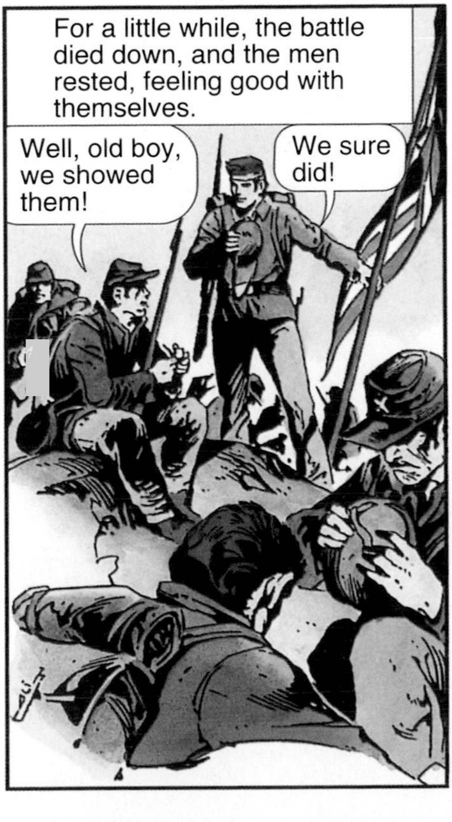
For a little while, the battle died down, and the men rested, feeling good with themselves.
Well, old boy, we showed them!
We sure did!

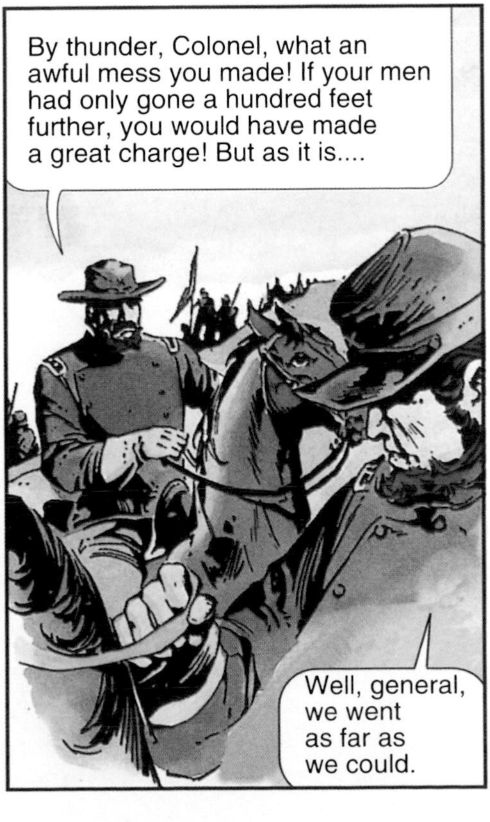
By thunder, Colonel, what an awful mess you made! If your men had only gone a hundred feet further, you would have made a great charge! But as it is....
Well, general, we went as far as we could.

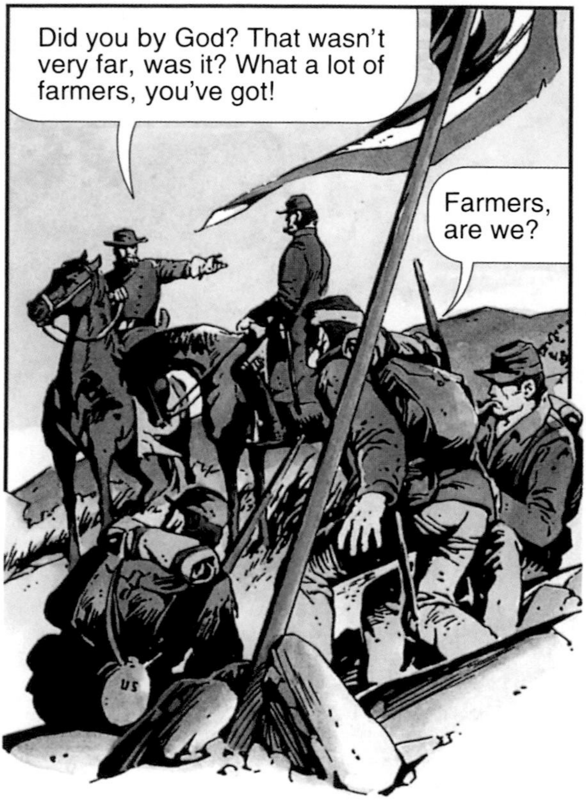
Did you by God? That wasn't very far, was it? What a lot of farmers, you've got!
Farmers, are we?

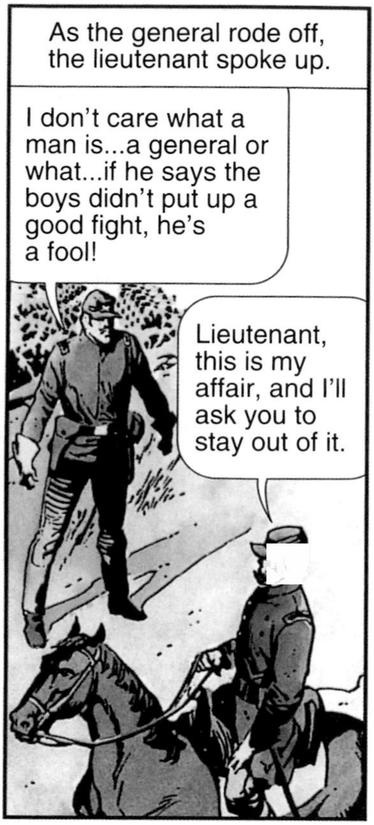
As the general rode off, the lieutenant spoke up.
I don't care what a man is...a general or what...if he says the boys didn't put up a good fight, he's a fool!
Lieutenant, this is my affair, and I'll ask you to stay out of it.

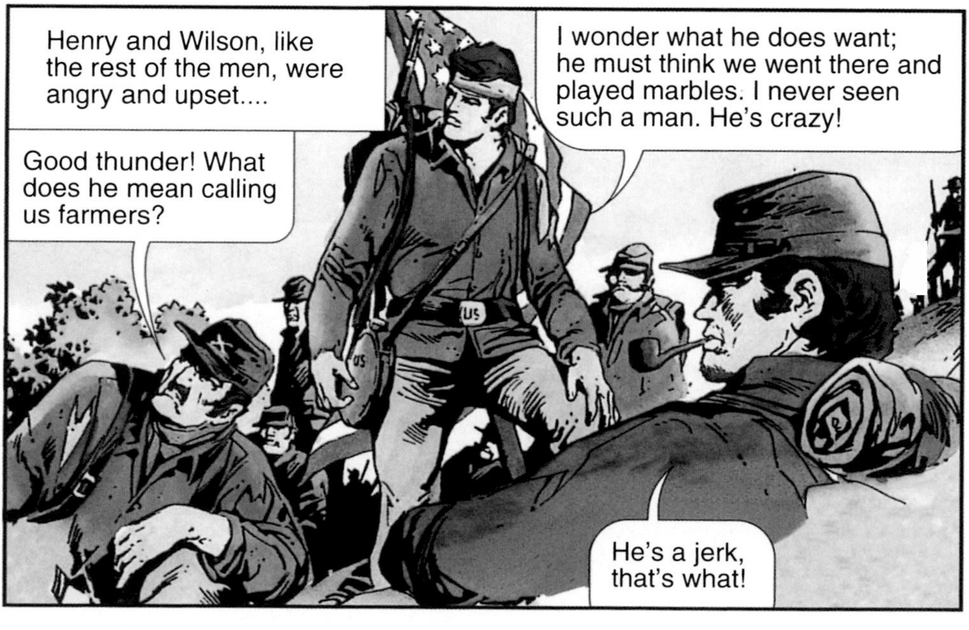
Henry and Wilson, like the rest of the men, were angry and upset....
Good thunder! What does he mean calling us farmers?
I wonder what he does want; he must think we went there and played marbles. I never seen such a man. He's crazy!
He's a jerk, that's what!

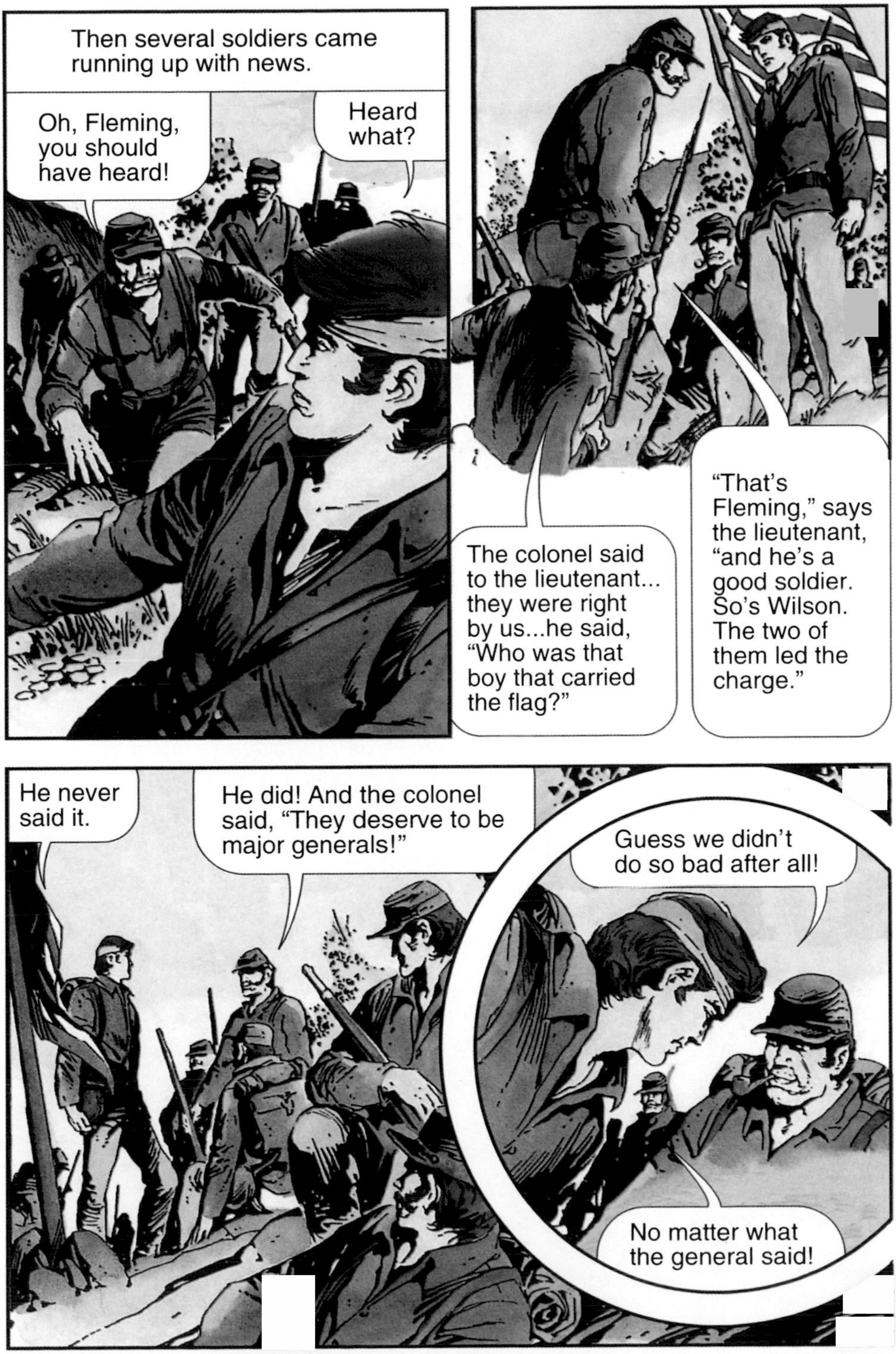
Then several soldiers came running up with news.
Oh, Fleming, you should have heard!
Heard what?
The colonel said to the lieutenant... they were right by us...he said, "Who was that boy that carried the flag?"
"That's Fleming," says the lieutenant, "and he's a good soldier. So's Wilson. The two of them led the charge."
He never said it.
He did! And the colonel said, "They deserve to be major generals!"
Guess we didn't do so bad after all!
No matter what the general said!

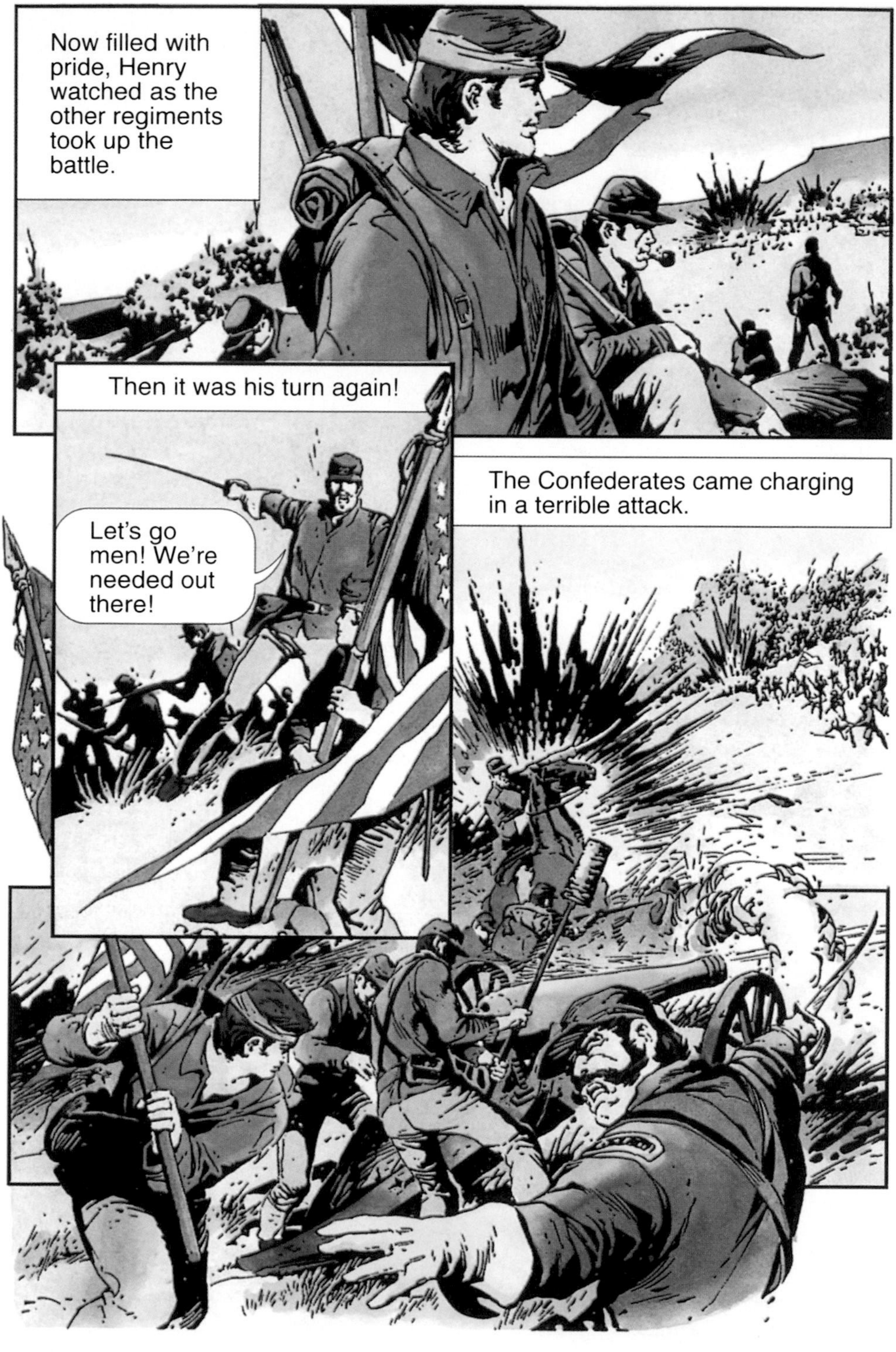
Now filled with pride, Henry watched as the other regiments took up the battle.
Then it was his turn again!
Let's go men! We're needed out there!
The Confederates came charging in a terrible attack.

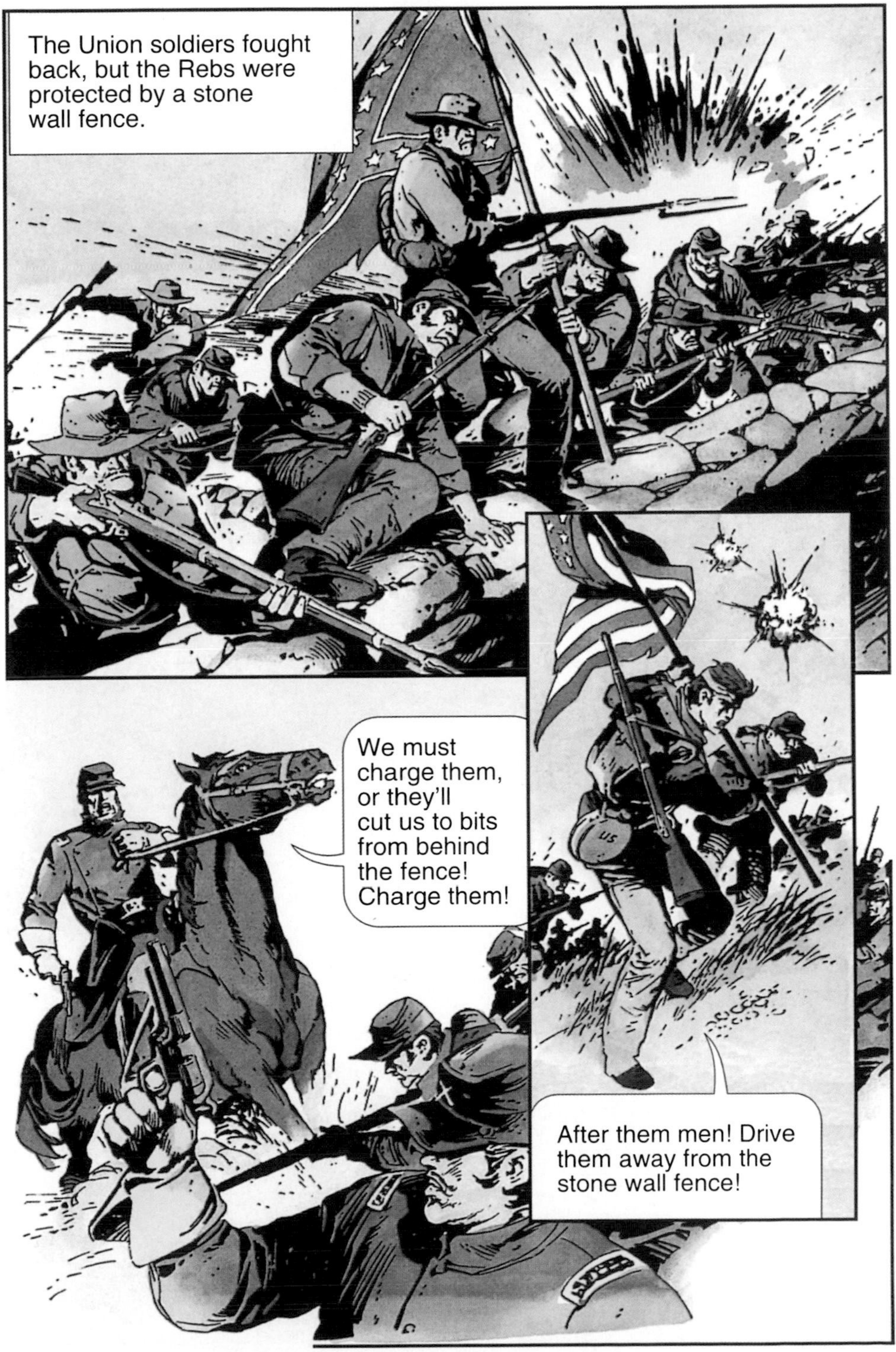
The Union soldiers fought back, but the Rebs were protected by a stone wall fence.
We must charge them, or they'll cut us to bits from behind the fence! Charge them!
After them men! Drive them away from the stone wall fence!

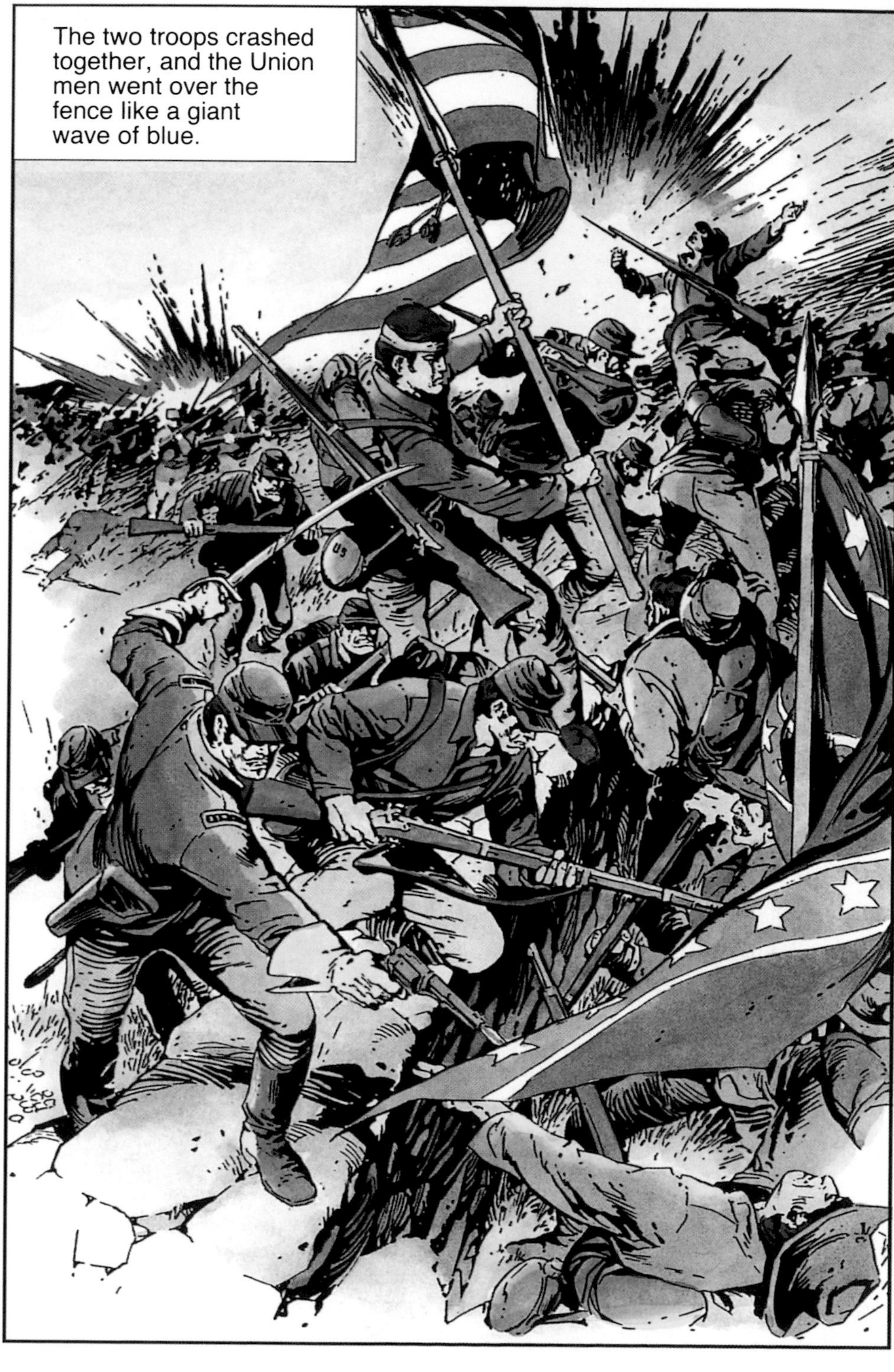
The two troops crashed together, and the Union men went over the fence like a giant wave of blue.

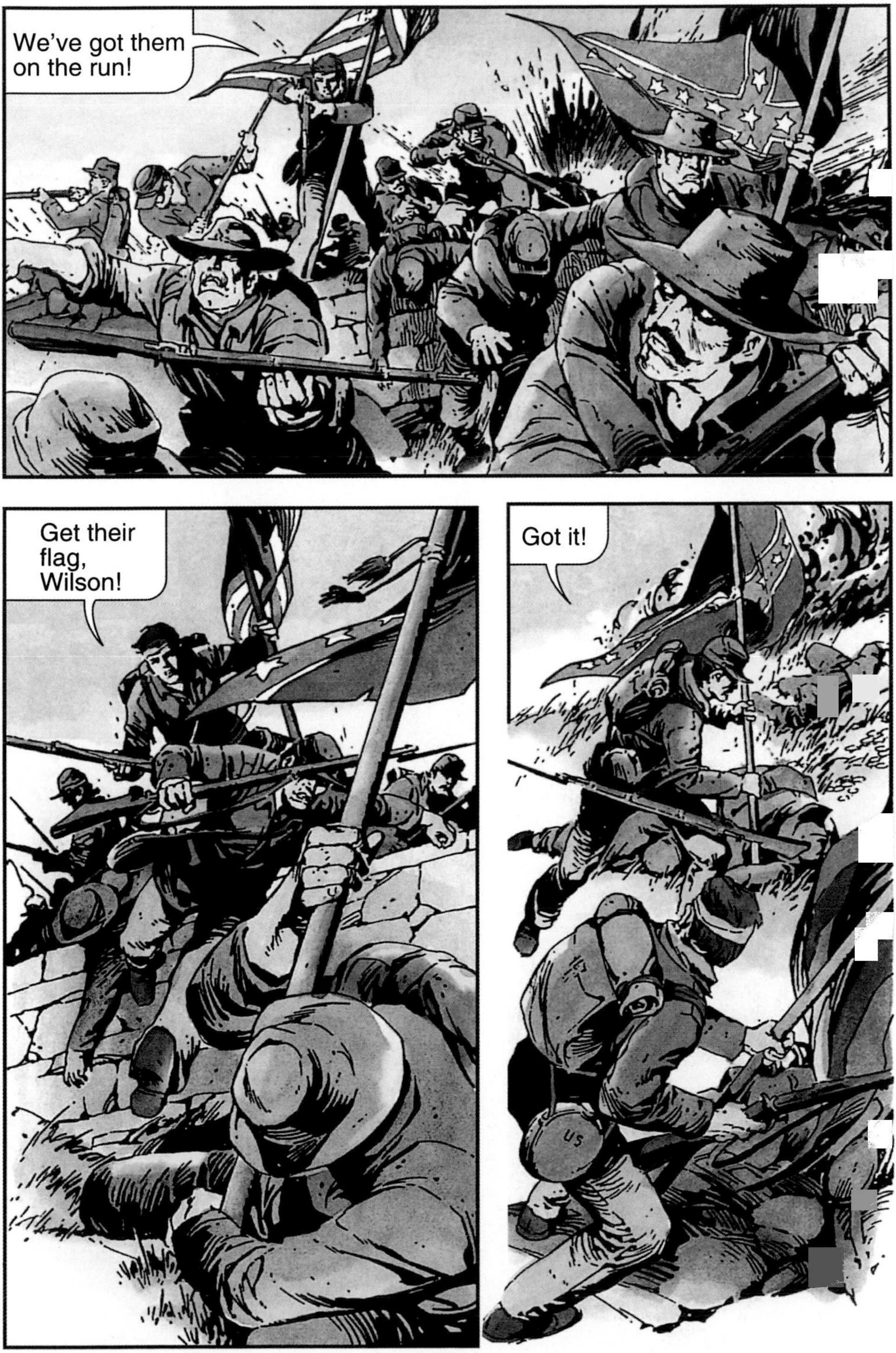
We've got them on the run!
Get their flag, Wilson!
Got it!

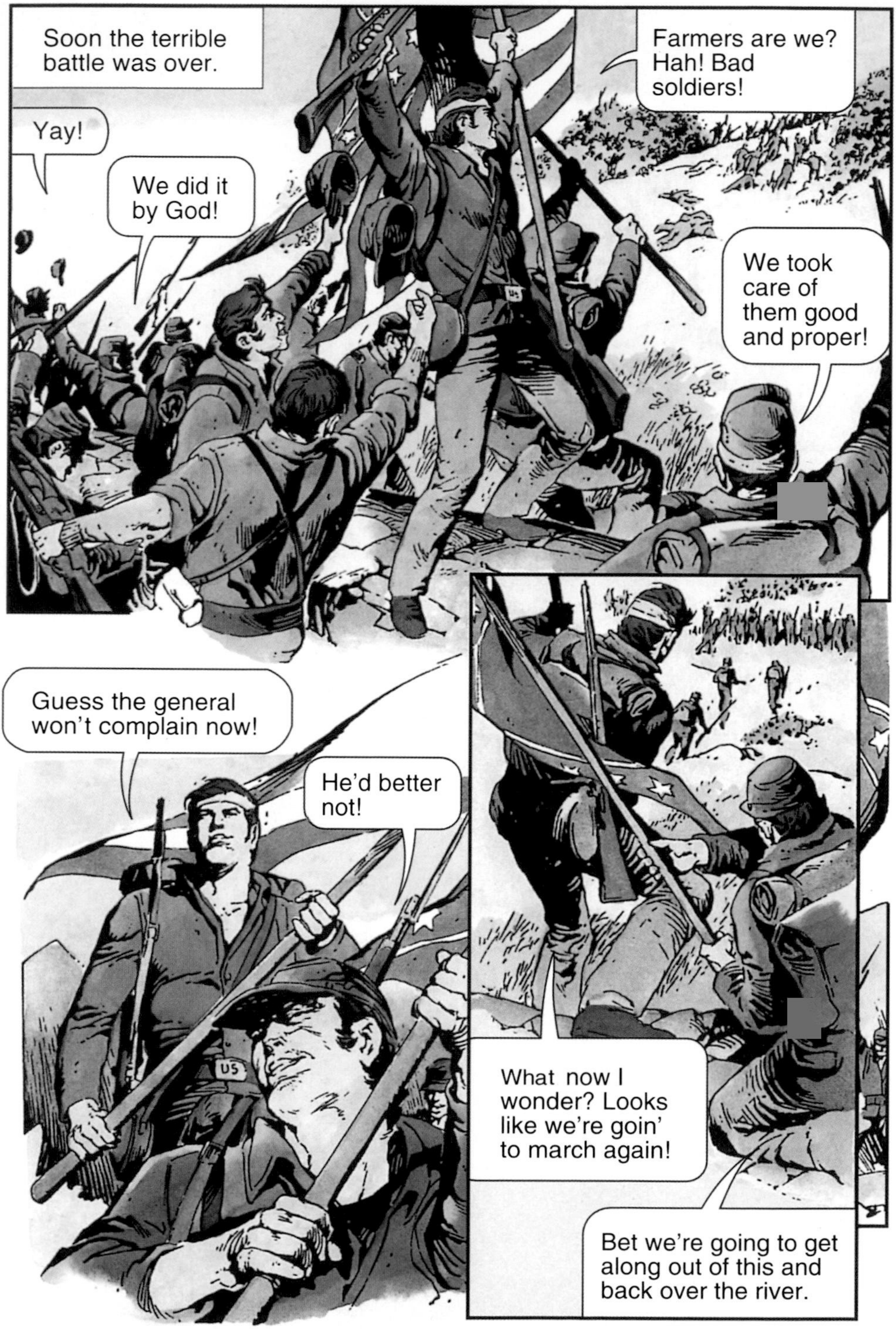
Soon the terrible battle was over.
Yay!
We did it by God!
Farmers are we? Hah! Bad soldiers!
We took care of them good and proper!
Guess the general won't complain now!
He'd better not!
What now I wonder? Looks like we're goin' to march again!
Bet we're going to get along out of this and back over the river.

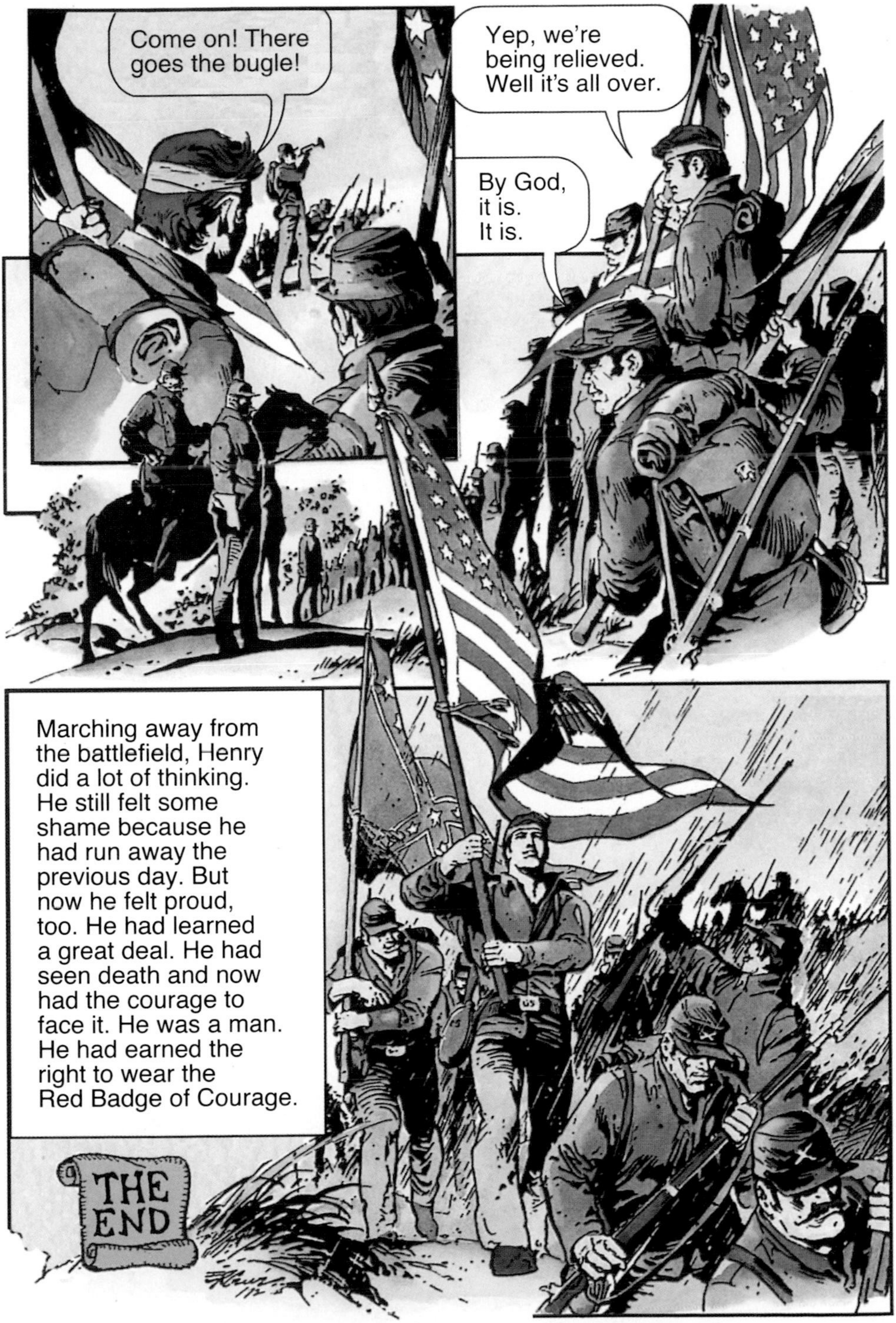
Come on! There goes the bugle!
Yep, we're being relieved. Well it's all over.
By God, it is. It is.
Marching away from the battlefield, Henry did a lot of thinking. He still felt some shame because he had run away the previous day. But now he felt proud, too. He had learned a great deal. He had seen death and now had the courage to face it. He was a man. He had earned the right to wear the Red Badge of Courage.
THE END